Also by CaSaundra W. Foreman

The Determination of I
The Motherless Children
When An Angel Takes Flight/The Light

Read It Again, Please!

❦

CaSaundra W. Foreman

authorHOUSE®

AuthorHouse™
1663 Liberty Drive
Bloomington, IN 47403
www.authorhouse.com
Phone: 1-800-839-8640

Published by AuthorHouse 4/16/2012

ISBN: 978-1-4685-7167-7 (e)
ISBN: 978-1-4685-7165-3 (hc)
ISBN: 978-1-4685-7166-0 (sc)

Library of Congress Control Number: 2012905614

This book is dedicated to:

*To the memory of my
Mother, Lorene D. Halstied Foreman
& Father, Clint W. Foreman, III
& my Grandparents*

&

*Anyone who is a grandparent,
aunt, uncle, sister, brother, godparent
or friend who helps make the difference
in the life of a child.*

These people are also known as the village.
***

For my children,
Marquis & LaBraska

It takes a village to raise a child.
~Attributed to an African Proverb

When I was a child, I spoke as a child, I understood as a child, I thought as a child; but when I became a man, I put away childish things.

~1 Corinthians 13:11

PREFACE

I had this thought late one night about all of the different people who are apart of children's lives, helping to mold and shape them into really responsible and productive members of society. These are the individuals who buy them educational toys just because they are special to them, or play games with them, or teach them how to tie their shoelaces, or tell time, or make scrambled eggs, ride a bicycle, or color inside the lines. These are the people who help them with difficult math problems and find books they will find enjoyable to read. These are the people who praise them for a job well done, attend their school programs and sports events. These are the people who fuss at them when they are misbehaving and encourage them when they are down. These are the people who remember their birthdays and do extra special things for them at Christmas. They are the ones who take them to eat ice cream and pizza and cry with the parents at all the big milestones in their lives.

I thought about all of the different people who influenced me, encouraged me and even acted as my parent, when my own parents weren't there. I recall how my godfather bought me a watch when I learned how to tell time, and how my uncle taught me to drive because I made my mother too nervous. I recall how my favorite aunt taught me to make scrambled eggs, and how my mother's friend scolded me once for opening the car door while the car was still moving. I remember all the people who attended the only pageant I ever participated in, and won. I recall how they cheered for me and took pride in my accomplishment. I remember how a family friend encouraged me when I was sad, and how another came to my rescue in a life and death situation. They added to all of the positive things my parents taught me.

They were the village, and I was a villager. They helped my parents look out for my best interest, and some of them are still doing it.

Although there are many parents, who don't want other people to say anything to their children when they are doing wrong, others gladly welcome help from grandparents, uncles and aunts, teachers, friends, church members and anyone else who imparts knowledge, positive behavior, encouragement and wisdom to help our future leaders learn to be respectful, responsible and productive.

I hope you enjoy *Read it again, please*!

Thank you for giving me an opportunity to touch your heart with words. May you be blessed beyond measure.

Miracles & Blessings!
CaSaundra W. Foreman

MAMA

It was rainy and cold that evening. It was November 1, and the leaves had fallen from the trees. The colors of red, green and yellow blanketed my lawn, although a few leaves had managed to hang on to their lifeline of the giant oak trees scattered around the front of my home. There were no squirrels running busily about, nor birds flying from limb to limb. There were no cars passing by, nor lightning flashing, or thunder rolling. It was quiet, as if the world had decided to give a few moments of silence for the occasion. The silent drops of rain that fell from the sky seemed to gently touch my window, making the ambiance perfect. Amazing how God created the scenery, and lack of background noises on that day, to match the sadness that was overshadowing me inside.

A mother should never have to endure the pain that I was feeling. I had cried so much, my eyes hurt. My eyes were swollen and red, and my voice had no spirit. My heart was broken, into what seemed like a million pieces. I wondered when the pain would end.

I knew that it wouldn't last forever. I was a Christian. I grew up in the Church. Went every Sunday, faithfully, come rain or shine. I sang in the choir, served on the Mission Board, and attended weekly services. I knew scriptures, so I knew that God would never put more on me, than I could bear. I knew that weeping would only endure for the night, and that joy would surely come in the morning. But my question was, "When, God, is the morning going to come?"

Martin was sitting at the dining room table. He had a letter in his hand and was looking at me, waiting for me to give him permission to continue. I was hesitant, yet I knew that I needed to hear, as well as understand, what the letter said.

"I'm sorry Martin. Read it again, please. From the beginning."

Martin looked at me with an impatient look. "Mama, maybe we should do this later. Maybe, this isn't the right time. You have had a long day, and so have I. I'm sure this can wait."

"No, Martin. It can't wait. This whole week has been one big blur. I can barely remember what the Preacher talked about yesterday during the funeral. I don't remember what the choir sang, and I don't know half the people who were there. I don't even think I ate yesterday. I haven't had an appetite."

Martin got up from the table, and walked over to the chair I was sitting in that looked out the window onto the front porch of my home. He kneeled down next to me, and gently placed his hand on top of mine.

"Mama, I know you are having a hard time dealing with this, so am I. But what did daddy always say? That this too shall pass. Everything will be okay Mama. I promise. It's still fresh. We will get through this, together."

I patted his hand softly. He was my youngest, and the most responsible. As I looked at him, I saw a few grey strands of hair popping up in the top of his head. He looked so much like his father; acted like him, too.

"Alright, Son. Go ahead." He reached up to wipe away a fallen tear from my face with his finger. "I'm ready. I guess. Read it again, please."

"Yes Ma'am."

He walked back over to the dining room table, and picked up the letter that he had been trying to finish for the past thirty minutes. He looked at me then took a drink from his coffee mug. As he put his reading glasses on and sat back down in his chair, he began to read aloud.

"Dear Mom,

I don't quite know where to start. I know that I haven't always been the best son. I have had some good days, and some not so good days. I want you to know, though, that I have always appreciated you, even when I didn't show you.

After Daddy died, you did your best to raise Martin and me. You made sure we didn't miss out on anything, and that we had the best of everything. You loved us, and prayed for us, made us go to church, even though we didn't listen to what the preacher was saying half the time, and supported us in everything we did. You attended all my football and basketball games, and I could hear you over everybody else in the crowd, no matter where I was, cheering for me, Laramie. That always gave me the extra push I needed to be the best.

When I went away to college, I had big dreams. I remember that daddy said for me to let my talent pay for my education. When I graduated, and became a coach, I knew you were more proud of me than I was of myself.

For the past few years everything has been perfect. I have had a perfect life, a perfect job, drove a perfect car, had a perfect apartment, and a beautiful, perfect girlfriend. Every aspect has been perfect!

Then, a few months ago, reality knocked on my door Mama. I went to the doctor for a routine physical, and a few hours later, I found out I was dying. The doctor said I have brain cancer. Brain cancer! Can you imagine, Mama, me, of all people, with cancer? I can't believe all the knowledge you and daddy made me soak up, and it is going to be my brain that kills me in the end. You know, it's funny how daddy used to say learning never killed anybody when I was in school. I thought about him when I got the news.

I got several opinions, Mama. All the doctors said the same thing, that within a few months I would die. They said I would experience excruciating headaches, and that my body would slowly begin to shut down. The bad part is that I had experienced headaches for months before I went to the doctor. I attributed them to stress from my job. Coaching and teaching have been very stressful the past several years, especially with all of the new guidelines for teachers, and the extra responsibilities coaches have, with keeping track of their players, and grades, and practice schedules. It's just hectic. I didn't pay attention to the warning signs my body was giving me when my vision started to change and I would lose my balance at times for no reason at all. I thought I was just being clumsy, but it was the tumor causing me to act that way. I didn't tell you, but I had begun to have seizures last year, but I didn't

3

realize that they were seizures until my doctor questioned me about my symptoms. I guess if I had listened to my body when it was trying to tell me something was wrong, I might have been able to beat this. Being a man, I think I just wanted to believe I was going through something that would go away. I never liked doctors, and you know I have always hated needles.

I am not bitter about my fate. I have accepted it. You and daddy taught us to pray about our situations and turn them over to God. That's what I did, Mama. I turned it over to Him. And, I am getting my affairs in order.

Mama, I have kept a secret from you because I knew you would be disappointed in me. I have to admit, I was disappointed in myself.

I have, children, Mama. You have grandchildren. Three of them and, I believe they all are still there in the City. Unbelievably, they all share the same birthday. I don't know how that happened, but it did. Yes, Mama, I was kind of irresponsible my senior year in high school. I didn't mean to be, but I somehow managed to end up in a relationship with three different young ladies, who were all so, different. When I went away to college, I thought I would keep in touch with them all, and figure out which one I really wanted to be with. I didn't realize that I had planted seeds of offspring.

When I came home for a break that Christmas, I went to visit these young ladies. I thought that two of them had gone off to college too. Yet, they were all pregnant. By me! I was so ashamed. I knew you would be angry with me. So, I didn't tell you, and went back to college, and came home less often. When I came home for Spring Break that year, I learned they had all had their babies, the week before, in March. Can you believe that? None of them knew about the others. I am surprised none of them ever came to see you. I am surprised that after seventeen years, you haven't run into any of them.

I ran into one of my high school teammates the last time I was home. He said he saw some students at the

High School who favored me so much they had to either be my children or kin to me.

I have thought about those young ladies often over the years. I have felt guilty for not helping them and for not acknowledging them. But now, Mama, I would like for you and Martin to find my children. I've left money for them, to help with college. I know this is bad timing, and that Martin is probably wishing I were there so that he could give me that look of his. But, everything happens for a reason.

I was young and stupid then, but I am a grown man now. I know I can't take back anything I did in my past, but I want to make things right for my children's future. I didn't look for them myself because I didn't want to appear in their lives for a brief period, only to disappear forever. My hope is that some good can come out of this, and that my children, your grandchildren, can get to know you, and Martin, and, maybe have a happily, ever after moment. I know this isn't a fairy tale, but I would like to believe that this mess that I have created could somehow have a happy ending.

Yes mama, I know what you are thinking. You wish I were there so you could smack me in the back of my head like you used to when I did something foolish. I know this would be one of those times when you would sit me down for a long stern lecture about responsibility and thinking first, and reacting later. I know this would be one of those times where you would have to walk away from me, to keep from slapping some sense into my thick skull. I can imagine the look of disappointment on your face, and I'm so sorry I am the cause of the disappointment and sadness you are feeling right now.

I am dying Mama. When you receive this letter, I will be gone. I want you to know I didn't tell you about the cancer because I didn't want you to worry. I stayed away from you after your birthday because I knew that my body was shutting down. I made Teresa promise not to tell you or anybody what was going on because I didn't want a pity party. I just wanted to live my remaining days as peacefully and proudly as I could. Knowing I have left money to help my children, although I don't know their names, makes me feel better, although not completely proud. Now, it's up to you and my baby brother to do what I never did, and that is be there for my children. Nurture them, influence them, love them and encourage them. Teach them about me. Tell them I am sorry I wasn't there for them. Tell them I was a good man, who loved to read books, and that my favorite books were written by James Baldwin, Langston Hughes and Alice Walker. Tell them my favorite thing to eat was Cookies and Cream Ice Cream. Tell them I loved Oreo cookies, and that I had to eat the middle first, and the outsides last. Tell them I ate so many Cool Ranch Doritos they made me sick to my stomach.

Tell them how I broke both of my arms twice. Tell them I was an honor student, and that I was so smart I could pass my classes just by listening to the teacher. Tell them I was number 16 in my class, and I went to college on a football scholarship, and became a High School Football Coach and History teacher, with the education I got from using my talent. Tell my children, Mama, that I ate ketchup on everything, and I used to stutter when I was younger. Show them my pictures, and trophies and medals. Smile when you talk about me, Mama. Don't be sad. Smile, that beautiful smile you smiled for me the last time I saw you.

Don't cry for me, Mama. I made peace with God. And, I know that everything is going to be okay. I love you and I appreciate everything you have done to help me become a man. I appreciate every scolding, every spanking and every time I got grounded. I appreciate you mothering me, and loving me because there are so many people who didn't have the kind of parents Martin and I had growing up.

I love you more than you will ever know.
Your Son,
Laramie Mitchell Wilson"

I recall just sitting there, staring into space. My mind was trying to grasp what I had just heard coming from my youngest son's lips, which came from my eldest son's heart.

Grandchildren?

Three of them?

All with the same birthday?

They would be seventeen years old now and about to graduate from High School. What in the world was he thinking?

"Mama, are you okay?" Martin asked, as he laid the letter on the dining room table.

I didn't know what to say. I could hear the rain starting to hit the window harder now. I could hear the thunder rolling, and I saw the lightning flashing. I could hear cars, as they drove past my corner, and their tires hit the puddles of water in the street. The silence was over, and it was time to right past wrongs.

Martin was an attorney at a local law firm. He knew at the age of eight he wanted to be a lawyer some day. When he realized how much money they made, and they got to talk in front of people, and wear the best suits everyday, he knew that was the job for him. As he grew older, some of the reasons for choosing to become a lawyer changed, but the drive was constant. He was class president in Jr. High and High School. He was on the student council, and volunteered within the community whenever he could. He said it would look good on his college applications. He graduated at the top of his class from high school and law school. He developed friendships with important members of the community and made lasting impressions on those he came in contact with.

Martin wasn't married, yet. However he was dating a young woman who was a social worker. The two talked about marriage, but because of their busy schedules, they just seemed to never get around to it.

Within days of reading the letter from Laramie, Martin had come up with a plan to find the children his brother had fathered.

Martin was more like my late husband than Laramie had been. He had a thirst for knowledge, but it didn't come easy for him. He, unlike Laramie, had to study hard. He struggled with math and science, but was persistent. He would often have to stay up late finishing homework he was having difficulty understanding.

Martin didn't like being the younger brother. He felt people were always comparing him to Laramie. One day, after the beginning of a new school year in the seventh grade, Martin came home and demanded that his father and I go to the school and have his classes changed. He said he didn't want to have any teachers whom had previously taught his brother. He said he wanted to form his own identity, and didn't want teachers to constantly compare him to his brother.

My boys were typical brothers growing up. They were born three years apart. They were alike in many ways, stubborn being one of them. Yet, they were also different.

While Laramie was outgoing in sports and could sometimes be characterized as a class clown, Martin was strictly about the books and wanted people to recognize his intellect. They both loved books. I guess it's my fault, because I loved to read. So did my husband. I believe my husband began reading to the boys the day they were brought home from the hospital. He would read anything, newspapers, magazines, encyclopedias, novels and anything with words that meant something. And he read the newspaper in the order in which it came, from front to back. He didn't skip around like some people do, looking for the Obituaries or the Sports sections first. He believed the way the newspaper was put together was in the order of its importance. He always said the world news was important so people could have a peek into the window of other's lives, and the local news wasn't as important to him because by the time the newspaper made it to our front door, the people in the community had already talked about it. He enjoyed the Sports section because it was there he said people got paid to do what they truly enjoyed, running around playing, like they did when they were kids.

My husband and I believed our sons had to have their own identities growing up, so after Martin was born, we moved into a three bedroom home, so they could have a room of their own.

Laramie's room was always a mess. He would take all day cleaning it up so that he could go to the movies with his friends on Saturday, and by the time he got back Saturday night, it looked like a tornado had hit.

The walls of Laramie's room were covered with posters of Michael Jordan, Larry Byrd, Patrick Ewing, Walter Payton, Joe Montana and Jim Brown. His favorite color was blue, so splotches of blue seemed to be all over his room. He had his own bookshelf, which contained Marvel comic books, and a collection of baseball, football and basketball trading cards. Most of the collection could be found scattered about the floor. He liked to read mysteries. He had his own collections of Donald J. Sobol's

Encyclopedia Brown's series, Gertrude C. Warner's *Boxcar Children* series, and Arthur C. Doyle's *Sherlock Holmes* that took up three shelves. He fell in love with a collection of books his father introduced him to by an African American mystery writer named Chester Himes. He also enjoyed reading books about history. Laramie's bookshelf also displayed a nice collection of trophies and ribbons from sports he participated in. On his bedroom door, was a sign that he had made at camp that proudly said, "Laramie's Room! Enter at your own risk!"

Martin, on the other hand, kept his room neat. He had a place for everything. He could tell by the way he arranged his things whether or not his brother had been in his room. Laramie would take Martin's socks because he was always losing his own. He had this story about how the washing machine ate his socks every week. Sometimes his father would get tired of hearing that story, and would go into Laramie's room and look under the bed, and find a mountain of socks that never made it into the washer. Martin fussed and ranted about his socks. He said Laramie always took the last pair of socks out of his drawer, and whenever he managed to get his socks back, they had holes in them. Martin was particular about his things.

Martin had posters of Dr. Martin Luther King, Jr., Jesse Jackson and Malcolm X on his wall. He had a picture of Thurgood Marshall taped to his door, with a sign underneath it that read, "My heroes all wear suits. This is my destiny!"

Martin had quotes of famous people taped to his walls. Dr. King's, "Life's most persistent and urgent question is, what are you doing for others?" and, "Our lives begin to end the day we become silent about things that matter." He had found a quote on a page in *Ebony Magazine* by Dr. King that read, "The ultimate measure of a man is not where he stands in moments of comfort and convenience, but where he stands at times of challenge and controversy." He had carefully torn it out of the magazine and bought a picture frame for it with money he had saved from his allowance. He hung it over the head of his bed.

His favorite colors were red and black, and he even tried to convince his father and I to let him paint his room red and black when he was in the fifth grade. Of course we said no, but I went out and bought him red curtains and a nice red and black comforter for his bed. The bookshelves in his room contained his own set of Encyclopedias. He had books about his heroes, the great Civil Rights leaders on his shelves. He read books about presidents and history makers. He enjoyed reading books about people who made a difference to our society and how their accomplishments were for the good of the people. He talked his father into purchasing for him two of Booker T. Washington's books, *Up From Slavery*, and *The Man Farthest Down*. When Alex Haley's, *Roots; The Saga of an American Family* came out, he did odd jobs for the neighbors so that he could buy his own copy. He inherited his grandfather's copy of Frederick Douglass's autobiography, *Narrative of the Life of Frederick Douglass, An American Slave*, which took Martin a while to read because he said it was so complex.

He kept the copy of *Incidents in the Life of a Slave Girl* by Harriet Jacobs in a plastic Ziploc bag because he said he wanted to preserve it's pages. My mother had given him the book from her own collection after he spent a few weeks with her one summer.

One of Martin's most prized possessions was a trophy he had won from an essay contest. That trophy was perched at the top of his bookshelf, beside the picture his father and I had taken with him the day he received the trophy. In that picture, Martin was wearing his first new suit. He was eight years old, and up until that time, he had worn his brother's hand-me-down suits. However, for that special occasion, my husband and I decided he needed a new suit. He was so excited that day.

"Mama, are you listening?" he asked, through the phone.

"Yes, Martin, I heard you," I replied.

"Well, what do you think?" Martin had called to tell me about his plan. He had decided the best, and easiest way to find Laramie's children was to set up a scholarship in Laramie's name, with specific guidelines, and an essay question. That way, because of the guidelines, we could narrow down quickly, which, if any of the applicants, were the children we needed to find.

"I...I guess that is one way of finding them. But, what if they all don't apply for the scholarship?"

"We will have to cross that bridge when we come to it. I have a friend who is a private investigator, and he is trying to locate some information about the mothers from the names Laramie gave me. Right now Mama, the scholarship idea is an easy way to find them, find out a little about them, and then, we can arrange to meet with them. This isn't just important to us, it's important to them because they have siblings they don't know about," he reminded me.

"I wonder how this will affect them, Martin. After seventeen years, the grandmother and uncle they never knew they had, appear out of nowhere, and give them money for college, left to them by the father they never knew."

"I don't know. But, it has to be done, and this is the least intrusive way to do it. It gives them the opportunity to contact us, and then, we can introduce ourselves to them, as their family. I am still working out the guidelines, but I am trying to make them as specific as possible, so that this process is simple."

"Ok, Martin. Whatever you think," I said, a little upset with Laramie for leaving this situation unattended to.

As I sat in my favorite chair with an open book in my lap, staring at the pictures of Laramie and Martin arranged above the fireplace, I silently asked God to see me through this time, and let it be an easy journey for us, as we attempted to find the children.

An ad ran in the local newspaper exactly four weeks after we buried Laramie.

> The L.M. Wilson Achievers Scholarship For Local High School Seniors. Guidelines: GPA of 3.0 and above, and born in March of 1989. Applicants must submit essay about themselves to be considered. Applications are available in High School Counselors office.
> Deadline for submissions: December 24, 2006
> Winners will be notified on, or before March 2. Please include a recent photo of yourself.

Martin said he paid a Jr. High school student fifty dollars to stand outside the high school and pass out fliers with this same information to the students after school one day.

He ran the ad in the community newspaper, the High School newspaper and posted flyers at the mall and all of the local teenage hangouts. He was friends with the local radio DJ, so the DJ made sure the scholarship information was announced several times each day until the deadline.

Martin was sure the right students would get the information.

It was December, and I was worried because Christmas was coming up, and it was football season, and basketball season had begun as well. There were so many other things going on to compete with our request from these local high school seniors. What if they didn't have time to write the essay? A thousand other "what ifs" ran through my head. I started feeling anxious. I knew all I could do was wait. But, waiting was the hard part. I had to pray, and ask God to give me patience. Out of all the things I had gone through with my children growing up, I believe the search for my grandchildren was the most challenging and enduring of them all.

One afternoon, I found myself sitting in the parking lot across from the high school scanning the faces of the children who exited the building. I was curious to see if any of them resembled my son. I saw a girl who looked like me when I was a teenager, but shook my head. It was probably just my mind playing tricks on me. A few minutes later, I saw another young lady walking with her friends who looked like my son. Tears immediately formed in my eyes, as I put my car in reverse, and backed out of the parking lot and headed home.

The news that Laramie had brain cancer was shocking to me. I was angry with him for not telling me he was ill, and I tried to remind myself he was a grown man, so he had to make the grown man decision not to tell his mother about his illness. He was right. I would have worried about him. I would have cried when he told me, and probably every day afterwards. I would have encouraged him to seek other opinions, but most importantly, I would have prayed for him and with him. I already prayed for him, and Martin, daily anyway, but I would have prayed specifically for his medical condition and his state of mind if I had known.

If only I had known. I would have taken a few more pictures of him at my birthday dinner, but he insisted on just the three, one of just he and I, one of just he and Martin, and the one of the three of us together. Just three. That's all. And, he was so handsome that day. But, now that I think about it, he did look a little pale, and sickly. His eyes weren't dancing like they had always done, since he was one-years old and had begun to get into everything he could.

The private investigator had begun to gather information about the young ladies that were the mother's of my son's children. I began to pray for the children daily. Even though I didn't know their names, God knew who they were.

That Christmas was hard. It was the first one without my husband and Laramie.

The boys had always been excited about Christmas. They used to sneak underneath the Christmas tree every day, looking to see which gifts had their names on them, and shaking them to see if they could detect by the sound of the package, what was inside. They were a mess.

My husband and I always bought them something they wanted, something they needed, and something we wanted them to have. My husband believed books were always good gifts for children, and so, every Christmas they got, in addition to clothes and toys, a new collection of books to add to what they had already read. Sometimes, my husband would ask the boys if they had read the books, and if they said yes, he would ask them what the book was about. If the boys couldn't give him enough information about the book to convince him they had actually read it, he would look at them and with his deep, tenor voice say, "Read it again, please, so you can tell me what you got from it." My husband believed every book had a main purpose for being written, and once a reader was able to realize what that purpose was, then they had gotten their monies worth out of it.

After my husband, Laramie Sr. passed I continued the tradition of buying books for my son's each Christmas. As they got older, they began to find books they believed I would enjoy and give them to me for gifts.

The week before Christmas, I managed to encourage myself to put up the Christmas tree. It was after Sunday dinner, and Martin and his girlfriend had just cleared the dinner dishes.

"Martin, will you go up to the attic and bring the Christmas boxes down?"

Martin looked surprised. "I thought you weren't going to put the Christmas tree up this year? You normally put it up the day after Thanksgiving."

"I wasn't in the mood, but Christmas is going to come whether we have a tree up or not, and I have never let a Christmas pass without waking up Christmas morning to the lights on the tree, and a nice Christmas breakfast. Your brother's death has taken a toll on me, but knowing that I have grandchildren somewhere lets me know there will be many more happy Christmases to come. And, someday, you and Simone may have children of your own."

Simone smiled at me, and looked at my son. "I'll help you bring the boxes down," she said, as she got up from the sofa.

As we spent the next two hours decorating the tree, and transforming my living room into a holiday dream, so many memories began to fill my mind.

I remembered last Christmas, when Laramie and his girlfriend, Teresa, were there. The two had announced they were planning to set a wedding date sometime in the upcoming year. However, Laramie passed away before they had the opportunity to make plans. We had so much fun that day. Hmmm…as I think back, I believe everything was so perfect that day. Maybe it was too perfect.

"Mama is this angel crooked?" Laramie asked.

"No, it's just fine, Son. It's perfect."

"The investigator believes he has found information on two of the women Laramie may have fathered a child with."

"That was a nice way to put it," Simone said.

I smiled. Martin was so business minded all of the time. I guess it was the lawyer in him.

"I gave him the yearbook from Laramie's senior year, and the names he'd left for me with some other information. He is going to let us know something by the end of the week."

"That sounds good, Laramie."

"We have gotten a few responses to the scholarship information we put out. I haven't opened the envelopes yet. I thought I'd wait, and maybe we can go through them next week, when we come for Christmas dinner."

Christmas dinner followed by pictures and information about children who were possibly my grandchildren. I sighed. "That sounds fine."

I went shopping with my sister. I found myself walking out of the bookstore with more books than I needed. Out of habit, I had purchased books for Laramie. The thought didn't cross my mind that he wouldn't be there for Christmas until I got ready to wrap the books to put underneath the tree.

Tears rolled down my face. Traditions are like habits, hard to break. My oldest wouldn't be with us for Christmas this time. His laugh, his smile, his voice, the sound of his snoring as he stretched out in the middle of the living room floor to watch the football game, wouldn't be with us. And I was truly saddened.

I wrapped the three books I had bought, and decided to give them to his children, whenever we met.

MARTIN

My brother always did things my mother didn't know about, but somehow, I always found out about them.

When we were teenagers, he would sneak out of the house after Mama went to sleep, and sneak back in before she woke up the next morning.

We were close, and although he made me promise not to tell mama he was dying, I felt guilty for keeping it from her. I prayed twice as hard for him after he called me that day in late August, after getting his third doctor's opinion. It was one of the saddest days of my life, and only the second time in my life I had seen my brother cry.

He came to my office, which was down the street from the doctor's office. As he walked through the door, I could tell by the look on his face something was wrong.

"Hey little brother," he said, as he extended his hand to shake mine. That was something we had learned as boys from our father, men should always shake hands and speak when entering a room. This simple act of cordiality had made us both stand out among other young men as we grew up. Our father always taught us in order to get respect, we had to give respect, and as young men, the more respectful and intelligent we were, the more doors and opportunities would be opened for us.

"What's up L?" I asked him. His hands were clammy. As we sat down, I behind my desk, and he in a chair normally occupied by my clients, there was a moment of silence. "You want some water, a juice or soda?"

"Yeah, a Pepsi would be good right now." He got up, and walked over to the small refrigerator I kept in the corner of my office, and helped himself to a Pepsi, and a Snicker from the candy bowl on top of the refrigerator. As he stood there, leaning against the bookshelf, his eyes scanned the room. Not really stopping on anything in particular, his eyes seemed to dart from object to object. His eyes seemed to tear up a little, as his gaze rested on mom and dad's wedding photo that sat on my desk. He quickly brushed away a tear rolling down his cheek.

The first time I saw my brother cry was when we were at my father's funeral. He was fifteen, and I had just turned twelve. Our father died in his sleep one night after attending one of my brother's basketball games. It had been a great game, too. Laramie scored thirty-three points and was the high scorer for the night. Dad was so proud of him, and when we went to eat pizza after the game, dad laughed and joked the whole time. He talked about how good of a player he used to be, and how he once dreamt of playing professional basketball, but chose to become a history professor instead. He talked about always having a game plan and a backup plan. A game plan was temporary, and for the moment. But a backup plan would see you through, after the game was over.

Our father was always saying stuff we didn't fully understand, but as we got older, and situations came up that reminded us of things our father would say, we understood and appreciated the wisdom he imparted to us. Mama always said our father was the smartest man she had ever met. She said he not only had book sense, but common sense too.

When Mama came to my room the next morning to tell me my father died in his sleep, I cried so hard I began to hyperventilate. But L just went outside and started shooting baskets. He stayed outside the whole day, making shot after shot. He didn't eat, just shot baskets until Mama made him come inside. The next day, which was Sunday, and the first time I could ever recall not going to church, L got up again, and without saying a word to anyone, went outside and spent the day shooting baskets.

Mama cried.

I cried.

Family and friends who visited cried.

My brother didn't. He just kept to himself and shot baskets. Later that night, after all the company had gone home, and the last few pieces of fried chicken had been put to the side just in case my brother decided he wanted to eat, L came in my room, looked at me and said, "5,506!"

"5,506 what, L?" I asked, confused. He was drenched with sweat, and extremely musty. He hadn't bathed since that Friday night after his game, and I was a little annoyed with him for making my room smell bad.

"5,506 baskets little brother. That's how many I made yesterday and today."

"That's a lot L."

"Yea, it is. It's the number of days I had dad in my life, too," he said, as he walked out of my room.

There were a lot of people at my father's funeral at the New Zion Baptist Church that Wednesday morning.

My mother's eyes were red from crying so much the days following my father's death. I had stopped crying, remembering my father's directions to my brother and I, should anything happen to him. He'd said, "Son, when my time comes, that God should see fit to carry me Home to my mansion in the sky, don't cry tears of sorrow on my behalf. Be strong for your mother, take care of her, and always respect her. Be responsible young men, who use your intellect to get you where you want to go in life. If you must shed tears, let them be tears of joy, in remembering the good times."

L had managed to keep his composure for four days. But when the lady at the church began to sing daddy's favorite hymn, during the final viewing of the body, L broke down and cried.

> *"I don't know about tomorrow.*
> *I just live from day to day.*
> *And I don't borrow from the sunshine*
> *'Cause the skies might turn to grey.*
>
> *And I don't worry about the future*
> *'Cause I know what Jesus said,*
> *and today I'm gonna walk right beside him*
> *'Cause he's the one who knows what is ahead.*
>
> *There are things about tomorrow*
> *That I don't seem to understand*
> *But I know who holds tomorrow*
> *And I know who holds my hand."*

I had never seen my brother cry before then. Not even when our father or mother spanked him. He took his licks, then went to his room and closed the door.

His composure in my office that day made me nervous. I started thinking the worst, but didn't want to jump to conclusions.

"Um, is everything ok?" I asked him, while trying to keep my wits about me.

He tore open the candy wrapper and started eating as he continued to lean against the bookshelf next to the refrigerator. As he began to say something, the telephone rang.

I pressed the DO NOT DISTURB button, and turned my chair to face my brother.

He looked a lot like our father. I looked more like mama.

"Lil brother, I found out today that I am," he paused for a few seconds, then continued, "I am going to...I am going to die." His voice trailed off, and his tears became heavier than before.

I just sat there, in my seat. Frozen. "What do you mean? You are going to die? We all are someday. It's our destiny." I was wondering if he had been drinking or something. But he didn't look like he was intoxicated.

"No lil' brother. I...I need you to listen for a minute. You see," he walked back over to the chair in front of my desk, placed the Pepsi on my desk, leaned forward with his elbows on his knees, and his chin in his hands, and said, "I found out two weeks ago I have brain cancer. Today I went for my third opinion, and he confirmed it. I only have a few months to live little brother. A *few* months."

I couldn't believe what I was hearing. "L, I don't understand. You seem healthy and look fine. What doctors have you seen? We can get another opinion. Obviously, someone has made a mistake..." I began looking through my contact numbers for my doctor friends.

"Martin, it's okay. I have been trying to figure this out for the past two weeks. I have seen the three best doctors in the area. They have all come up with the same diagnosis. It's my time, to go. I have to just accept it, and get my affairs in order." His tears came to a halt. Just as his began to dry up, my tears began to form.

I didn't want to believe what he was saying and in my mind, he was always the big, strong quarterback brother, who was an amazing athlete, with the prettiest girlfriends, and lots of friends. He never got sick when we were kids. He just managed to break his arms a couple of times, sprain his ankle, and dislocated his knees every few months.

"I haven't told Mama, and I don't plan to..."

I cut him off, "What do you mean Laramie? Why wouldn't you tell her?"

"Because I don't want her worrying and fussing over me. You remember when daddy died how depressed she got. You remember how she worried when grandma had a heart attack, and Grandpa developed lung cancer. She takes on everyone's problems and let's them consume her, and she becomes sick herself. So, I'm just going to be a man about it, and just let her love me while I…finish the rest of my course. I don't want her pitying me. I just want to see her happy dancing cocoa brown eyes smiling at me and feel her natural motherly love embrace me. I don't want a pity party Martin. I threw one for myself when I first found out, and it didn't change anything."

"What about Teresa? Does she know?"

My brother got up from the chair, and walked over to the window. As he looked out, an airplane slowly flew by. It was sunny that day, but cool.

"I haven't told her yet. I needed to come see you. With my fate being given to me, I have some business to discuss with you."

"Do you have a will?"

"No, and that's what I need to discuss with you…and something else. Now, since you are my brother, and my lawyer, I trust that you will keep this conversation between us."

"Laramie, you know my job binds me to be confidential."

"Well, I need you to help me get my will in order, and…I need you to find my kids and get them the money I am leaving for them to help with college."

"YOUR WHAT?" I asked, looking at my brother as if he had lost his mind.

"My kids Martin. I have at least three. My senior year in high school, things kind of got out of hand. And…well, from what I understand, I have three kids here somewhere. That's why I never moved back here to teach and coach. I couldn't face the fact I might be teaching one of my own children I never acknowledged or took care of."

"Does mama know?"

"Of course not. I'm surprised neither of the girls contacted her. I have a yearbook that has their pictures in it. I will get the information together for you to help you locate them, and the kids…my kids, who should be seventeen-years old now."

"L, how did you manage to keep this a secret for seventeen years?"

19

"I don't know. But I have thought about them and their mother's everyday. I felt like less than a man, knowing our father took care of us and helped mama raise us. And when mama does find out, which won't be until after I am buried, she just might try to bring me back from the grave so she can slap some sense into my head," he smiled.

As hard as it was to do so, I smiled too. I was not happy at all about keeping two big secrets from mama. But, my brother had made up his mind about what he wanted, and how he wanted it done.

"It might be in your best interest for you not to let mama know you knew about this either. I'd rather her not be angry with you for following my wishes."

"Does Teresa know about the kids?"

"No," he said, as he sighed heavily. "Teresa and I talked about having children. Well, she talked, and I mainly did a lot of nodding and listening. I don't think I'm going to tell her either. I'm not sure she would understand, and I don't want to have to deal with any unnecessary drama right now. I would love to just live the remainder of my days in peace."

"I understand. You need to write your will, and make your special instructions and provisions very specific so there is no misunderstanding once you are…once you are gone. I will do my best to see your instructions are carried out and I will find your children." I reached into my desk drawer and pulled out a form for my brother to sign.

As he turned from the window, and walked over to the chair in front of my desk, I handed him a pen and slid the paper towards him.

"There's one more thing. I am leaving money to help you take care of mama. You and I have always shared the responsibility, and with me dying, it will all fall on you now. Daddy told us to make sure we took care of her, and I want to do my part, even after I'm gone."

"L, you shouldn't be worrying about this right now. Mama will be taken care of. You need to just worry about you." I turned my head away from him so he couldn't see the tears that had begun to fall from my eyes. Real men don't cry so I'd been told. But my father taught us real men do cry when the ones they love the most are going through something we can't help them out of. He said our tears allowed the pain we felt to ooze out of our bodies, and although it didn't change the way we felt completely, it made our hearts feel just a little better.

When we were kids, my brother and I didn't talk much. We became friends after our father died. Mama made us spend a whole weekend with each other because we seemed to fight all the time. We had to stay in one room. Whatever we did had to be done together, unless it was going to the bathroom or taking a shower. If I wanted to watch TV, we had to agree on a show. If he wanted to go outside, he had to play with me. We weren't allowed to have any company that weekend, or talk on the phone. My mother was determined that the two of us would be friends, not just brothers.

"Your family is your blood-line," Mama said. "Nobody is going to love you or appreciate you like family. Brothers need to get along, and love each other, no matter what. When it's all said and done, family will rush to the hospital to see about you and sit in the waiting room all night, pray for you when you can't pray for yourself, remember you on your birthday, remember your faults and laugh at your jokes and sit on the front row at your funeral."

After he left my office that day, I closed the door behind him, and sat in my office and cried. I cried because my big brother was dying, and there was no way for me to fix it for him. I cried because I knew my mother would be hurt by the death of my brother. She always said children should bury their parents, not the other way around.

I looked over the instructions my brother left for me, and I knew he'd put a lot of thought into his plans. A few months were all the doctors said he had left. I guess when you know your time on earth is drawing near you can set things in your life in order. Not everyone has that opportunity.

The next few weeks were hard. My brother lived two hours away, so I made sure we talked at least several times every day. He decided to turn in his resignation to the high school. He said he didn't want to start the school year off with the team, only to leave them in the midst of football season. His desire was to do some of the things he'd never gotten around to doing because he was always too busy. Things like fishing, playing golf, going to the movie theatre, spending the day movie hopping and taking the two cruises he had won but never went on.

He waited to tell Teresa the news he was dying until after mama's birthday dinner in September. He said he didn't think Teresa could handle being around mama, pretending not to know Laramie was weeks away from dying.

My brother spent the week before mama's birthday with her. He hadn't told her he'd quit his job, he just showed up the Saturday before and surprised her by saying he had come to spend the week with her for her birthday. Mama was happy because Laramie had never spent more than one night with mama since he graduated from college.

He decided to spend time with mama because he wanted her to have special memories of him, to hopefully shed some softness to the hard days that were surely to come for her following his death.

He decided to get up each morning and fix her breakfast. He cleaned out the garage for her, and the attic. He dusted the ceiling fans and raked the leaves that had begun to fall in the yard. He painted the outside of the house for her so she could save the money she had planned to spend to get it done.

While he worked to set mama's house in order, he prayed God would let him go quietly in his sleep, the way dad had gone. He prayed his children would forgive him for not being a part of their lives. He prayed mama would be okay and not make herself sick with worry after his time had come.

Mama was so happy to have Laramie home. I knew why he was there, so I let them have their alone time for the first couple of days. I went by and had dinner a few times that week with them, and we talked a lot about old times.

Laramie tried to keep his composure when he was around mama. He said the headaches weren't as bad as he was expecting, and the medication his doctor had given to help with the pain helped considerably.

At mama's birthday dinner, which would be the last family moment we had, I realized that my brother was deteriorating at a fast pace. As strong as he was around our mama, he was struggling to maintain his secret. I saw him stumble several times that day.

Four weeks after mama's birthday dinner, L called me to say that it was almost over. I jumped in my car and drove the two hours it took to get to his house in less than an hour. I guess God was with me because there were no cops on the highway that day.

I don't even recall parking my car. I just remember running up the steps to his apartment and using my spare key to let myself in.

He was lying on the leather sofa in the living room watching Monday night football. The Cowboys were playing the Chargers. He was wrapped up in a blanket. Although it was warm in the room to me, my brother was freezing.

Teresa wasn't there. She had run to the store to get him some Cookies and Cream ice cream. He didn't really want the ice cream. He just didn't want her to be at the apartment when he closed his eyes for the last time.

"You made it lil' brother. You made it," he said, as the Cowboys fumbled the ball. He reached for my hand, and I extended mine to him, for what would be the last time I would shake my brother's hand.

"Yeah, I made it L. I probably broke about twelve traffic laws, but I had to get here." I sat down on the floor next to the sofa where my brother lay stretched out.

For a moment we just sat there watching the game. As the Cowboys scored a touchdown, he grabbed the remote from the coffee table, and turned the TV down.

"I love you lil' brother, and I'm proud of you."

I turned to look him in his eyes. There was only darkness in them where light used to be. "I love you too L, and I promise to do everything I can to find your children."

He smiled at me, and nodded his head. "I know you will, that's why I didn't trust anyone but you to do it. Can you get my Bible off of the bookshelf over there for me please?"

I got up from the floor and walked over to the bookshelf that contained every book he had acquired from the time he learned to read, until now. Books our father had given him, the comic strips, and the first edition of Howard Fast's *Freedom Road*. There were rows and rows of knowledge amidst the shelves in my brother's apartment. Some of them he had reread, and allowed friends to borrow. I smiled to myself when I saw a picture of the two of us when we were kids in a picture frame. I must have been about a year old, and he was just three. In the picture my big brother was sitting in dad's big comfy recliner, with me sitting in his lap, reading to me.

I found the Bible on the top shelf and walked back to the sofa.

"Open it."

As I unzipped the cover, I found several envelopes inside. Each one had a name handwritten on the outside. I looked at him.

"My final words lil' brother. My last thoughts for the one's I love the most. I've had a lot of thinking time these past months and I found myself needing to put some thoughts on paper. Please give mama that letter for me after the funeral. And…Teresa too." His breathing became shallow. But he took a breath and spoke again. "I went to visit daddy's grave when

I stayed with mama that week of her birthday. I hadn't been out there since I graduated from college. I know people say your loved ones stay with you in spirit when they pass on. But I kind of felt bad that I hadn't visited his resting place in a long time. Do me a favor lil' brother?"

I looked at him. "Anything L."

He managed a grimacing smile through his pain. "Come visit me every once in awhile. Don't forget about me when I'm gone. I know it sounds strange, but come talk to me out there, at my resting place. Come let me know how mama's doing, and how the search is coming with my kids. Let me know when you and Simone finally get married and when you have kids of your own. Just in case I don't get to make it to Heaven...and my spirit doesn't get to be free because of the sins I have committed, come check on me. Can you do that for me?"

"L, you went to church just like I did growing up. So if there's anything you need to get right with God, now is the time to do it! Ask God to forgive you for whatever it is."

"I have lil' brother. I have. But just in case, you know, everything that preacher said about God forgiving us isn't exactly true, and just in case my sins are too big for God to forgive, I just want to know that you will come visit me."

"There is no sin God can't forgive if you ask with a sincere heart. God loves you. Mama and daddy taught us that. Remember daddy used to say that there are no big and no little sins. Sin is sin in God's eyes. So whatever it is, God will forgive you for it. I will come visit you. That you can believe. I think you need to pray one more time before..." I looked over at him and his eyes were shut.

"L!" I yelled his name. But he didn't speak. I looked at him. He was still breathing. He suddenly opened his eyes.

"Hey lil' brother, I'm good. I was talking to God like you suggested. Can you read that scripture to me. The one they read at daddy's funeral... about the seasons..." his voice was getting weaker.

I was finding it harder and harder to maintain my macho composure. Trying to be strong for my big brother was not an easy task. I wished mama were here. She would know just what to say, and just what to do. She'd probably stroke his forehead and sing to him the way she used to do when we were kids.

I managed to find the scripture he was asking me to read from the book of Ecclesiastes 3:1-8:

"To every thing there is a season
And a time to every purpose under the heaven:
A time to be born, and a time to die;
A time to plant, and a time to pluck up
that which is planted;
A time to kill, and a time to heal;
A time to break down, and a time to build up;
A time to weep, and a time to laugh;
time to mourn, and a time to dance;
A time to cast away stones, and a time to gather
stones together;
A time to embrace, and a time to refrain from embracing;
A time to get, and a time to lose;
A time to keep, and a time to cast away;
A time to rend, and a time to sew;
A time to keep silence, and a time to speak
A time to love, and a time to hate;
A time of war, and a time of peace..."

When I finished, my little brother whispered, "Read it again, please, lil' brother…just one more time…" as he closed his eyes.

With tears streaming down my face, I began again, *"To every thing there is a season, and a time to every purpose under the heaven: A time to be born, and a time to die..."*

By the time I finished, my big brother had finished his course, and was resting in the arms of God. He no longer felt pain, or had to wrestle with the worries of this life.

I was glad I was able to make it to my brother's apartment so he could leave this earth with a member of his family who loved him by his side. I'm glad my brother, my friend was at peace, and went to glory with a smile on his face.

Teresa arrived a short time later with a pint of Cookies and Cream ice cream to find the paramedics outside the apartment. She was too late to say goodbye.

I'd actually started looking for my brother's children before he passed away. The private investigator I hired had been able to locate two of the women, but I hadn't contacted them yet.

I was kind of nervous about the task that had been given to me. I wondered if the children would be receptive to mama and I, and to my brother's gift. I wondered if they would be angry with us because my brother never acknowledged them until after his death. I wondered if the children would be bitter, having grown up without their father in their lives. I wondered if the children would be appreciative and if they actually had plans to attend college. I wondered if they had been well taken care of and if education had been a priority to the people who raised them. I wondered if they had been loved and nurtured, the way mama had loved and nurtured us throughout our lives.

My life was hectic after my brother shared with me that he was dying. I hated having to keep his secret from mama and from Simone. Having to keep that secret between my brother, God and myself was stressful.

My relationship with Simone was suffering because I couldn't share with her what was going on. She wasn't used to me not talking and she was struggling with my moodiness. She wasn't used to me not paying attention to her when she talked to me about her day, and she wasn't used to me missing dates we had scheduled months in advance. As bad as that seems, I even forgot to send her flowers on the anniversary of our first date.

I prayed more during that time than I had ever prayed before. I prayed for my brother to be healed, and if not physically, spiritually and emotionally. I prayed for guidance in finding his children. I prayed my relationship with Simone wouldn't suffer and that my mother wouldn't have health problems after receiving the news that my brother died.

When we were children my parents made us pray every night. They made us pray for each other, for our family and friends, and they taught us to ask God for forgiveness of our sins. My father would remind us that every good and perfect thing comes from God, and that only God can heal us, deliver us, bless us, comfort us and forgive us of our sins.

One night after my father passed away, I walked past my brother's room and saw him kneeling down beside his bed. Mama had taught us that we should be humble enough to kneel down before God when we prayed out of respect for Him.

I heard him whispering this prayer to God:

"Dear God, please forgive me for rolling my eyes when daddy fussed at me about my homework and for wishing that he wasn't my daddy. I know it's my fault that he died because I kept asking you why you picked him to be my daddy. I loved him, he was just so hard on me sometimes. Please forgive me for not listening to mama when she tells me what she thinks is best. I promise to listen to her and appreciate her. Please don't let her die too. Bless my brother and me. Amen."

My brother blamed himself for our father's death. He believed that his disobedience and disrespect of our father caused God to take him from us.

The envelopes came into my office within days of each other. There were three of them. My heart skipped a beat as I wondered if the right kids had actually sent us their information.

I looked at the return addresses on the envelopes as they came in and matched them to the addresses the private investigator had given me for the women he believed were the mothers of Laramie's children. Two of them matched. The third address was promising because it was hopefully the lead to the third child the private investigator had not been able to locate.

Christmas was a few days away. Mama called me everyday to find out if there was any news about the kids.

Simone and I managed to work things out after my brother's funeral when I finally broke down and shared with her all I had been keeping to myself.

I believe we were all looking forward to Christmas dinner, and the hope and promise a new year brings to God's people who have faith that God will always work things out.

LARAMIE

Dear Martin,

I just wanted to tell you I love you and I am glad you are not only my brother, but also my friend.

I remember when you were born. You were so little, Mama had to carry you on a pillow when she brought you home from the hospital. I used to watch over you like I was your bodyguard, because you were my little brother.

I used to read to you before you learned to read. I remember how we used to get up on Saturday mornings and watch *The Bugs Bunny Road Runner Show, Hong Kong Phooey, Scooby Doo* and *The Teenage Mutant Ninja Turtles*. We used to love watching *The Three Stooges, The Little Rascals* and episodes of *Fat Albert* when we could catch them.

We used to fight over the prize in the box of Lucky Charms and CoCo Puffs until mama started buying us our own box so we could each have a prize.

I remember how we used to play with Legos and tried to build the models on the front of the boxes. We were a great team.

I remember how dad used to take us to the movies on Saturday afternoon, and how he used to take us fishing.

I used to enjoy watching *Star Trek* and boxing with him. I missed him so much when he died.

I recall how we used to fight over the drumsticks

at dinner when mama fried chicken. And I laugh when I think of how we used to draw straws to see who was going to lick the bowl with the cake batter after mama made a cake.

We used to have the best birthday parties. Chili dogs, chips, Cookies and Cream Ice Cream and chocolate cake. And we'd play kickball and football with our friends after we ate.

I remember when we had our first fight, over who's turn it was to mow the lawn, and how mama made us spend the weekend together, so we could learn to be friends.

I remember how we used to drink up all the Kool-aid and leave just a little drop in the pitcher in the refrigerator, and mama would get mad and make us drink water for the rest of the week.

I remember watching the *A-Team* and *Knight Rider* on television and wishing that we had cool cars like the guys on TV. Remember when I asked mama if I could cut my hair like Mr. T's? I knew she was going to say no, but it didn't hurt to ask.

I loved having water balloon fights and eating the frozen Kool-aid popsicles that mama made for us on hot summer days.

I remember wishing when we got in trouble that mama would spank us instead of dad because mama's licks didn't hurt. I remember how you used to hide dad's belt when you knew you were going to get a spanking, and how he always found it.

I thought it was cool how dad used to come home after work, and the first thing he would do was give mama a kiss. I remember watching them slow dance at night to that Etta James song, *At Last*, when they thought we were asleep. I remember how dad never let a day go by that he didn't let us hear him tell mama he loved her. Nor did a day go by when he didn't tell us that he loved us and was proud of us. I recall you asking him one day why he always said he was proud of us, and he told you he was proud of us because he knew one day we were going to be successful men who were positive members of society.

I smile when I recall how you became your own person, and didn't want to walk in my shadow. I was proud of you when I heard you tell our parents you didn't want to have any teachers I had because you didn't want them comparing you to me.

I remember how you used to come to my basketball and football games, and read a book. My friends used to say you were a nerd, but I always corrected them and told them you were smart and had big dreams and plans.

I remember waking up on Christmas morning. If I woke up first, I woke you up so we could go look at our presents under the tree together. And if you woke up first, you would come wake me up. I remember how Aunt Myrtle gave us socks every year. We always knew what we were getting because she didn't try to wrap them in a box. She just wrapped them up, however they came. I remember when dad started giving us books every year, and how he would make me reread them if he felt like I couldn't tell him what the book was about. I used to get so upset with him for doing that, but as I got older, and school got harder, I understood why he made me do it.

The situation I got myself in with the girls was crazy and irresponsible, I know. But as I became more of a man, I knew I had to make things right.

About a year before I found out I had cancer, I took out an insurance policy. I know it was God's guidance that led me to do it because I hadn't even thought about life insurance. I just figured I was young and had a long time to worry about dying. A friend of mine is an insurance agent, and he started telling me how much insurance I could get for a small amount of money.

I thought about it, and knew if nothing else, I could leave the money to my kids. I decided I was going to try to find them, so I could be a father to them, if they would let me.

Then, things started happening. I met Teresa, and well, now here we are.

I know you felt bad keeping secrets from Mama, but it was for the best.

When I'm gone, take care of mama, check on Teresa every once in a while, and love my kids the way I should have.

The five hundred thousand dollar life insurance policy should be enough to take care of mama, and split between my kids. It should be put in a trust, to be distributed by you, for their education, and whatever you see fit.

I trust you will do what you feel is right.

Remember me, especially when you eat a big bowl of Cookies and Cream Ice Cream or some Double Stuff Oreo Cookies.

You turned out to be an outstanding man, and dad would have been proud of you.

You know, I still get down on my knees at night and pray, just like dad and mama taught us when we were kids. When I found out I had cancer, I got on my knees several times a day. I begged God to hear my prayers, and let me be healed.

Then, one day God let me read a story about a man who died in a horrible car crash and left his wife and six kids to mourn his passing. He had recently lost his job, his house was in foreclosure and he was on his way to the bank to apply for a loan to take care of his family until he was able to get back on his feet. He died unexpectedly and tragically trying to go get money to help take care of his family.

I realized I was dying, but had already been blessed with the mindset to get my affairs in order and would be able to say goodbye to those I love. That man's family was waiting for him to come home.

Perspective.

Putting things in perspective…we don't get to choose the hand we're dealt, but we can play the hand to win!

Dad taught me that many years ago, and I forgot about it until I read that newspaper article. I refused to feel sorry for myself, or be angry or bitter with God. He allowed me to live a good, happy life. For that, I have to be thankful.

Thanks for the memories. Thanks for helping me, after I'm gone. Your brother, L

*****

Dear Teresa;

I want you to know I love you very much. I thank God every day for blessing me with the opportunity to know you.

You have been such a positive asset to my life, and I am sorry we will never have the chance to see our dreams come to fruition.

I remember the first time we met. I'd seen you several times before, but I don't think you noticed me. You would come to the gym, walk on the treadmill for forty-five minutes while listening to your Ipod, head to the ladies locker room, and come out twenty minutes later, ready for work.

I hated the treadmill. It just seemed unnatural to me for someone to walk in place for a period of time, going nowhere. But, I wanted to meet you, so one day I made sure I got on the treadmill next to the one you always chose. I had gotten to the gym a little earlier that day, so that I could practice my poise on the treadmill before you came and stood next to me. I didn't want you to think I was clumsy when it came to that particular piece of exercise equipment.

Then, you came, and smiled politely at me as you stepped on the treadmill, ready to get your work out on. I was so bored after walking in place for ten minutes, and felt myself about to fall, but I couldn't catch myself. I had begun to daydream about you and, ended up making a fool of myself in the process.

I remember how you looked down at me, as I slid to the floor. You never stopped moving. You asked me was

I okay, but never missed a step. Embarrassed, I headed to the locker room. I stayed in there a while, hoping you would be gone when I came out so I wouldn't have to face you.

But you weren't, and when my eyes met yours, you caringly said, "The treadmill isn't for everyone. Maybe you should try running the track."

That was my cue, to win your heart, love you unconditionally and treat you with respect.

These past few months haven't been easy for me, and I know they have been equally as hard for you. When I told you I was dying, you took my hand, looked me in the eyes and said, "I'll walk through the valley with you…and someday, we'll meet again on the other side."

Now, I'm a man who has never been a crybaby. But you touched my heart that day. You let me know that you would be there until the end.

I knew this guy in college who got sick with leukemia his senior year. The girl he had been dating all through high school broke up with him when she found out because she said she couldn't stand the thought of losing him to death. Ironically, he didn't die, and is happily married now to a friend who stood by him during his battle.

I'm so thankful you chose to stay and see me through to the end. That's love, baby. That's love.

I saw the hurt in your eyes when I told you I had kept a secret from you. When I told you about the children I had, but have never met, I felt so small. But I didn't want you to find out from anyone else after I was gone. I wanted you to hear it from me, and know I am not proud of my choice.

I have prayed God will send you a good man who will love you, and take care of you and will treat you like the queen you are. I hope you will think of me from time to time, and think happy thoughts.

Please keep in touch with my family. Mama really likes you, and my brother says you have been good for me.

Don't be sad for me. God allowed me to live thirty-five years. Now, I'm going to a place, like the Bible says, where sickness shall be no more. And everyday will be Sunday.

I love you, much more than words can say.

Until we meet, again....Laramie

MYRACLE

Dear Scholarship Committee:

I love Cookies and Cream Ice Cream! I don't want any other kind. I used to think that Strawberry was great, but one day, my grandmother gave me some Cookies and Cream. She said, "Just try it, Myracle. I bet you'll like it." Since she had never given me anything that I didn't like, (other than black-eyed peas, sweet potatoes, okra, squash and asparagus) I tried it. I was four years old then. Ever since that day, Cookies and Cream has been my most favorite thing to eat. I really enjoy eating it with a few Oreos on the side. But I have to eat the inside first. Incidentally, I don't like the regular Oreos. They have to be Double Stuff. I mean, why pay the same price for just a little *stuff,* when you can get twice as much. At least that's what my grandfather says. I'm sure he was talking about something besides the filling inside my cookies, but it made sense to me.

My name is Myracle Michelle Lee. I am seventeen years old. I was born March 2, 1989. My mother was a freshman in college at the time, and I have never met my father. My grandparents raised me so my mother could finish nursing school.

I have no brothers or sisters, to my knowledge. I do have lots of cousins, because my mother has three brothers and two sisters. Mom was the youngest of my grandparent's six children. She was the only one of their children who finished college, and the only one of their children to have only one child.

My name, Myracle, comes from the fact that I weighed only 2 pounds when I was born. I was two months early, and the doctors told my mother that I might not make it. My grandmother prayed for me and said God told her I would be just fine. My mother, who was nervous about what was going on with me, decided to name me Myracle, because of something she had learned growing up at church. She said she'd always been taught to speak things as if they already are, and to have faith the size of a mustard seed. She wasn't too particular about the name Faith, but she did believe that it was a miracle that I was alive. She decided to name me Myracle so I would be blessed anytime someone called or spoke my name. She wanted my name to mean something, to stand out from others, and to represent God's blessing.

My grandfather visited the hospital every day, sometimes just sitting in the waiting room praying and waiting for me to show signs of improvement. My mother used to tell me she talked to me everyday. My grandmother came to the hospital to sing to me several times a week. She is a wonderful singer, and I've heard often from members of my family that the other babies in the nursery would stop crying when my grandmother began to sing as if they were being serenaded.

One night, when I was about three weeks old, I stopped breathing. One of the cords inside my incubator had gotten wrapped around my neck somehow, cutting off the ability for my tiny, struggling body to breath. My grandfather had come to see about me, and noticed that I was turning blue. He yelled for a nurse, who said that it was a miracle that he came along when he did. For some reason, the tube that was hooked up to me, that was also supposed to be hooked up to the heart monitor, wasn't. So no one knew I was in distress. It was a miracle, because my grandfather never came to visit me at night. He usually came during the daytime. This particular night, he said he was going to the store to buy a pack of cigarettes, and something made him keep driving to the hospital.

Needless to say, I made it through that storm and today I am a healthy, smart young lady, who has her mind set on graduating from high school.

I love to read. Ever since I can remember, I have always enjoyed books. When I was little, I used to climb into my grandfather's lap with a book in my hand. He would read to me, making facial expressions, and appropriate voice changes to go with the story. I hated for the story to end. I would always beg him to read it again, and again. Until, finally, he would tell me, "Just one more time."

My mother and my grandmother would read to me too, but they didn't read like my grandfather.

In elementary school, I read library books so fast that the librarian had to find new books for me to read. She encouraged me to read above my reading level because I'd read everything on my grade level. I read *The Little House on the Prairie* series, *Little Women*, *Great Expectations*, and so many others. I would hide myself in my room, and read for hours. Sometimes, when I ran out of books to read, I would reread something I had read before.

Because I love to read, school has always been easy for me. I am currently ranked number two in my senior class. I would love to be valedictorian, but my grandmother says God gives us what we need, and places us where He wants us to be. So, if I am number two, then I am satisfied. I really have never had to study much to be honest. I can pass a test just by listening in class. I mainly read for pleasure. My grandmother told me one day if I spent more time studying, and less time reading I probably would have been class valedictorian. It's funny. No one in my family enjoys reading, and they all have said they had to study hard in school.

I play volleyball and I'm on the track team. I am fluent in Spanish, and participate in the drama club. I am Senior Class vice-president and an ambassador for my school. I'm involved in various clubs at school, and I have earned two thousand and seventy five volunteer hours over the past three years.

I am also active in my church, where I sing in the choir, work in children's church and greet guests every other Sunday.

I love Cool Ranch Doritos. Although they make my breath needy of a toothbrush and toothpaste, they are my favorite food to eat, after Cookies and Cream Ice Cream, of course.

After I graduate from high school, I want to major in Education. I would like to be either an English teacher, or a History teacher. I hope I can make a difference in the life of some young person some day.

Thank you for your consideration of me, for this scholarship.

"I wonder what they will think of my essay Grand D. Do you think I should change it?" I asked my grandfather. I was so nervous. I wanted to win as many scholarships as possible to help pay for college. I loved writing essays, but this one was different.

"No Sugar, it sounds just fine to me. If they don't pick you for the scholarship, then it wasn't meant to be. You put your heart into that essay, so what God has for you, is what you will receive. Now hurry and print it out so we can get it in the mail," my grandfather replied, as he smoked his pipe. "It's funny how this scholarship seems to be specifically for you." He picked up the flyer with the information about the scholarship from the table. "I can't say I've ever heard of a scholarship set up for kids who were born in a specific month and year."

"I hadn't heard of it either, but it makes no sense for me to pass up the opportunity for free money. Now, which picture do you like best?"

I held up five different pictures I had taken recently. I wanted to send the picture in with my application that showed my personality the best. Of course I also wanted to send the perfect picture. The one with the cutest outfit and my best hair moment was a must.

"I like all of them Myracle. Those people won't choose you by how you look. They will choose you by your grades and how smart you are. Beauty don't have nothing to do with it." He was watching the news and shaking his head at the news report of Saddam Hussein who was on trial and being sentenced to hang. "O wee. Those people over in that country sure have a way of punishing people for their crimes. The electric chair and gas chamber are one thing, but hanging. Umm. Umm. Umm. That sho' is a way to go." He turned his attention back to me, and said, "Did you make up your mind yet Sugar?"

"I guess Grand D. This one is my favorite." I had selected the picture I took at homecoming. I looked like a supermodel that day. "I wish Granny would get back from the store. I'm starving," I said as I placed my essay and photo in the envelope and sealed it up. "Grand D, where do you keep the stamps?"

My grandfather got up from his comfy leather recliner and limped over to the antique desk in the corner of the living room. The desk had belonged to my grandfather's grandfather, who was a slave on a plantation in Mississippi. His name was Ezra, and he had built the desk when he was twenty-four years old. Ezra was killed trying to save one of his son's who was drowning in a flood. The family had managed to pass the desk down from generation to generation. Grand D said when I got my own place the desk would be passed down to me.

Growing up, I wondered who my father was. I wondered if I looked like him. I wondered if my eyes were the same color as his, or if my nose was shaped like his. I wondered if he would have loved me and been proud of me. I wondered if he knew about me. I wondered if he was smart and if I got my love of books from him.

I used to ask my mother questions about him. What was his name? Where did he live? What did he look like? Would I ever get to meet him?

I asked her if she had pictures of him and if she knew his phone number so I could call him.

My mother always seemed to dismiss my questions. She never talked about my father. She told me one day when I was about twelve years old that when I was old enough to understand, that she would tell me about my father.

I asked my grandmother questions too. But she was no more help than my mother. Eventually, I stopped asking, but I never stopped wondering.

My mother and I weren't real close. Even after she finished college, I continued living with Grand D and Granny because it was where I was comfortable. My grandparents seemed a lot more loving than my mother, so I felt more at peace with them.

My Uncle Terry was my favorite. He taught me how to ride my bike, how to skate and how to make Rice Krispy Treats. He picked me up from school everyday, and was the most patient when it came to teaching me how to drive. Grand D said I made his heart beat fast whenever he let me drive and Granny said I made her nerves bad. I didn't think my driving was bad. I hadn't hit anything but a few curbs.

My mother didn't have the patience or the time to practice driving with me. But sooner or later, I was going to get my license and that would be proof I was a good driver.

I had a couple of best friends in school. We spent a lot of time together but all had different goals. My friend Sherice wanted to be an actress, which would be perfect for her given her dramatic character. And my friend Gammy wanted to be a lawyer. We all wanted to go to different colleges, but we all agreed we would live in the same city after we graduated from college.

Both of my friends have a dad and mom in their home. Sherice has a big brother and Gammy has twin little sisters. My friends felt I was the luckiest of the three of us because my grandparents spoiled me. That was their opinion. I didn't think I was spoiled. My grandparents had always gotten me whatever I asked for. Grand D used to tell me anything I wanted, just ask for it.

I didn't ask for much, but I seemed to have everything I needed and more.

I loved to come home from school to the aroma of Granny's cooking. Ever since I was a little girl, my granny would always have a glass of milk and four Double Stuff Oreo cookies waiting for me on the table when I came in from school. I would sit at the table and do my homework, or read a book while granny cooked dinner. Grand D would help me with my homework, or read to me everyday.

Things hadn't changed much, now that I was seventeen. I still came home from school to find a glass of milk and four Double Stuff Oreo cookies waiting for me on the kitchen table, and the aroma of granny's cooking throughout the house. I no longer did my homework at the kitchen table because I had my own computer in my bedroom.

Every night I prayed for my family, and for the father I never met. I prayed to God to bless me with scholarships to pay for college, and I prayed for the relationship with my mother to get better.

My Uncle Terry told me once that my mother loved me, she just didn't know how to show it because my father broke her heart before I was born. He said she became depressed after I was born because she felt as if she wouldn't be able to accomplish her dreams. My grandparents told her they would raise me. My mother let them.

Sometimes I worried about my grandparents because of their health. Grand D had really bad arthritis and coughed a lot. Granny made him go to the doctor when he began to cough a few months ago, and the doctor told him he needed to quit smoking. Grand D said he'd been smoking since he was fifteen years old, so he couldn't imagine what he would do with his free time if he didn't smoke. I worried about lung cancer because the commercials on television always talked about how smoking caused cancer. But Grand D said he wasn't worried about cancer. He said that he was going to die of something eventually, whether it was naturally, from cancer or because of his bad heart. So, he was going to enjoy life while he could and deal with death when it knocked on his door.

Granny had high blood pressure and migraine headaches. She took a lot of medication everyday. I prayed every night God would bless them with good health and that they wouldn't die because I couldn't imagine living with my mother.

ADMIRE

"Mom, can I borrow the keys to your car so I can mail this package?" My fingers were still typing as I tried to multitask. As usual, I had waited until the last minute to finish something important. I was like that with my schoolwork. However, what I was working on wasn't schoolwork. It was an essay for a scholarship for college. Something I desperately needed.

"Did you finish the essay Admire?" my mom asked from the living room.

"Almost finished. I'm just proof reading it. I hope I said enough, but I'm not sure."

Mom came into my room, and sat down on my bed. "I'm sure it's perfect Admire. You have always been good at writing essays. So this should be a piece of cake. Would you like me to look over it for you?"

"If you don't mind." I was really nervous about the essay. I was good at writing, but this essay was personal, and for strangers. Strangers who would be deciding if I would receive money to help pay for college. It would be the tenth scholarship I had applied for.

Mom and I switched places, as she sat in front of my computer desk and began to read aloud.

"To Whom It May Concern:

As a child, I grew up loving books. My mother started reading to me from the time I was conceived, up until I was old enough to read to myself. I could sit for hours, and listen to the stories from the hundreds of books that graced the shelves in my room. I recall my uncle reading to me.

42

I would climb into his lap, and make myself comfortable as he took me to far away places and far away times with words and pictures. When he would finish, and close the book, I would look at him, with big brown eyes, and say, "Read it again, please." And, he would, until I fell asleep.

My name is Admire Mychel Johnson, and I am a seventeen year old high school senior. I was born March 2, 1989. My mother, who is a teacher, raised me with the help of my grandmother. I have never met my father.

Some of my favorite things are Cookies and Cream Ice Cream, Cool Ranch Doritos, Double Stuff Oreo Cookies and of course, books.

My name, Admire, comes from the quote that my father wrote in my mother's high school yearbook, "You always admire what you really don't understand." My mother said my father was a very smart and intelligent man.

Until last year, I was an only child. My mother recently married a man who has two children from a previous marriage.

I am very active in my school. I am in the choir, a cheerleader, on the student council and an honor student. I am currently ranked number one in my senior class. I volunteer every weekend at the nursing home, reading to the residents. I also have volunteered my time at the Family Abuse Center, babysitting the youth in the summer for free.

I am active in my church as well. I am a lead soloist, a vacation bible school teacher and a praise dancer.

I plan to attend college next fall to work on a degree in criminal law. I have wanted to be a lawyer ever since I was a little girl. I enjoy watching television shows that have law themes.

I also enjoy reading books about crime, and mysteries. I love books by John Grisham, Chester Himes, Walter Mosely and James Patterson.

I enjoy helping people and have always been taught that we should be a blessing to others, and God will bless us in return.

I look forward to meeting you, and I hope you choose
me to receive the L.M. Wilson Achievers Scholarship."

"Mom, what do you think?" I asked, trying to read the expression on
her face.

"It's fine Admire. It says just enough, without saying too much. Now
which photo did you pick to send with it?" She looked at the stack of
photos on my desk. She smiled as she looked at each one, recalling the
occasion of which it was taken.

"I'm undecided. Maybe you should pick it," I said, putting on my
shoes. I had about twenty minutes to print out my essay and get to the
post office.

"I like this one," she said. "It shows your charming personality. Besides
that blue outfit you're wearing has always been one of my favorites." Mom
handed me the photo she selected and I placed it in the envelope with the
essay. Looking at the clock on the wall, I kissed her on the cheek, and ran
towards the car, grabbing her keys off the kitchen counter on my way.

I loved my mom. She was so down to earth and understanding. She
was mean when she had to be, but I was a pretty good teen.

I had recently gotten my driver's license. My stepfather had taught
me to drive.

I made it to the post office three minutes before it closed. I saw that
girl from school, Myracle, walking down the street. My friends thought
she and I looked alike. She was mailing something too.

As I pulled out of the parking lot, and headed back home, I became
distracted by the radio. A song had come on I didn't like, so I looked down
to change the station. When I looked back up an eighteen-wheeler was
headed for me. I couldn't move.

I was so cold. My body was aching. I couldn't speak, or open my eyes.
I couldn't move. I was frozen inside my body.

I could hear my mother. She was crying. What was going on? I heard
her praying.

"Lord, please let her be fine. She's so young...too young to die..."

I heard my stepfather trying to comfort her. My Uncle Vincent and
Meemaw were in the room too. I heard the sounds of a heart monitor.

O my goodness! I was in the hospital! I remembered. The eighteen-wheeler! The radio! O God! I'm too young to die!

"God, please let me be fine. I don't want to die yet. I want to graduate from college and help people. I want to have a family of my own. I want to take the mission trip with the church and I want to give my valedictorian speech. Please God. Let me wake up!" I felt a tear roll down my cheek. Somebody's hand wiped it away. It was a rough hand, so it must have been Uncle Vincent. I heard him reading to me earlier from the James Patterson book that I had recently started.

"God, I'm not ready to die. I want to live! I have to live! You said in your Word that if I have faith the size of a mustard seed, that I can move mountains. Well, God, I have faith enough to believe this is just a test of my faith, of my family's faith. I am strong enough to come out of this. I will get those scholarships that I applied for. I will be just fine. I am fine. I am fine. I speak life over myself. I am healed. I am healed. God, I am healed."

Another day passed. I was still in a coma.

"God, did you hear me? Did you hear my prayers? Did I do something wrong? Did I pray wrong? Why am I still here? Why am I still in this coma? Help me God, please! I'm sorry for sneaking out of he house a few times to see my boyfriend. But God, all we did was talk. Please God, don't punish me for being sneaky, and for being disobedient by seeing my boyfriend, even though my mother told me I couldn't."

I heard my stepbrothers whispering to my stepfather.

"Is she going to die?" Jonathon asked.

"Can she hear what we are saying?" Andrew asked.

"No, she isn't going to die, and yes she can hear you. So say something positive. Say something to make her happy. Say something funny, so she can laugh at you like she always does." My stepfather was a nice guy. He was good to my mother and me. Jonathon was fifteen and Andrew was ten.

"I don't like seeing her this way Dad," Andrew said. He was the goofy one. He was always coming up with goofy jokes. He could change his voice to sound like any movie character and wanted to be an actor when he grew up. He was also a class clown at school, and his dad received plenty of phone calls from teachers.

"She will be just fine Andrew. Admire is a fighter. She is fighting right now to come back to us. Any day now, she will sit up and talk to us. She and Jonathon will be debating over some current news issue and those pretty brown eyes will make us all smile again. Have faith." My stepfather was trying to sound reassuring.

Hours past. I heard my mother praying beside my bed. She was sobbing, but she was praying harder than I had ever heard her pray before.

"Lord, I ask you to give my daughter back to us, in able body, sound mind and beautiful spirit, the way she was five days ago. I'm not ready to let go of her yet. When you gave her to me, even though I wasn't ready to be a young, single mother, I made the choice to keep her. I made the choice to love her, raise her, teach her, protect her, nurture her and impart your wisdom in her. I have raised her to be a responsible, respectful, intelligent and beautiful young woman. She has so much to share with others. She has so much still to experience in life. Please, Lord, allow her to continue her course. Don't let her time be up Lord. I know I sound selfish Lord. But I love her. She's my baby. I'm not ready to let go of her. And...I don't know that I can live without her. Give her back to me Lord. Please hear my cries Lord. Please hear my cries."

A tear rolled down my cheek. She must have been looking at me, because I felt fingers gently brush the tear away.

"Admire, I need you to fight. You have always been a fighter. You fought to keep your grades up when they said you had dyslexia. You got over that disability and now you are going to be valedictorian of your senior class. You are a fighter. You fought to be cheerleading captain. You fought to help your Meemaw beat cancer. You fought to have your room painted purple. You are a fighter. Now, fight to come back to me. Fight, Admire! Fight!"

I was fighting. But it seemed like my fight was useless. God wasn't ready for me to come back. At least not right then.

The next day, I heard the nurse talking to my mother. Telling her I was a very pretty girl.

"She reminds me a lot of my daughter," the nurse said.

"How old is your daughter?" my mother asked.

"Seventeen. She's a senior this year."

"Admire is seventeen and a senior too. I'm sure they know each other. This is a small town so all the kids in school know each other. What's your daughter's name?" my mother asked. She talked to everybody. People she knew, people she didn't know. She made friends easily. So did I.

"Myracle. Myracle Lee."

"Myracle? Myracle. That's the name of the young lady the police said pulled Admire from the car before it caught on fire! Was that your daughter?"

"It could be. She didn't mention it to me. She lives with my parents. I will have to call her and find out," the nurse said, sounding surprised.

"I'm sorry, I didn't introduce myself. My name is Valerie Moore," my mother said. "What's your name?"

"Alicia Lee. You look familiar Valerie. Did you go to high school here?"

"Yes. I graduated in '88."

"So did I. I guess we look a little different after seventeen years," the nurse said, as I heard noises coming from the machines next to my bed.

"Yes, I kind of remember you now. Weren't you a cheerleader?" my mother asked.

"Yes. All four years of high school. Well, it's good seeing you," she said as she headed out the door.

"It's good seeing you too. Could you please find out if your daughter Myracle was the one who pulled Admire out of the car? I would love to meet her and thank her in person."

"I will call her and let you know. And please, don't give up hope. Your daughter is going to pull through this. It just takes time," the nurse said as she left the room.

I heard Meemaw singing beside my hospital bed. She sung to me for a long time. Then I heard the ladies from her mission group come in. They were praying for me. I felt people all around me. They must have formed that prayer circle Meemaw always talked about. With this much prayer going on for me, something good was bound to happen.

Uncle Vincent believed in lucky numbers. His lucky number was seven. He always played the number seven when he played his lottery numbers, even though my grandma told him gambling was a sin, and he was going to hell. My uncle won quite a bit of money with his lucky number seven, so it didn't bother him when grandma scolded him. He'd just laugh and hand her a wad of money and tell her to put it in the collection plate at church for him. My grandma would look at him and say, "You can't pay God to keep from going to hell."

"Maybe not, Mama, but I bet Reverend Tatum sure won't mind seeing that blessing in the collection plate." They'd both laugh.

On the seventh day I lay in the hospital, Uncle Vincent came into my room and said, "Admire, this is your day. You have been here for seven days, and since seven is my lucky number, you need to open up your pretty brown eyes and talk to me. It's been too quiet around here, so go ahead, and make me smile. Open your eyes, move a finger, pass gas, do something." He stood next to my bed rubbing my hand.

My uncle always made me laugh, and this morning was no different. I managed to smile, and move my finger.

"There you go Princess. Now, open your eyes for me. Let me see your pretty brown eyes."

"H-e-y...U-n-c-l-e," I said, as I opened my eyes.

"Hey little Girl! Thank God! I was beginning to think you were trying to miss out on giving that valedictorian speech you've been working on since your freshman year. You surely must have had one long talk with God." He was smiling at me, and pushing the button to call the nurse at the same time.

"Yeah, Uncle, you could say that God and I have had quite a conversation. I remember the truck coming at me, and then I kind of blacked out. I have been able to hear bits and pieces of conversations when people come in my room, but how long have I been out?"

"Today would have been day seven. I keep telling y'all that seven is my lucky number. And this just proves it."

The nurse came into my room to check me out.

"Where's mama?" I asked. "And, why can't I feel my legs?"

My uncle and the nurse looked at me and then at each other.

"What's she talking about?" My uncle asked the nurse.

"I am going to have to call the doctor. Can you get in touch with her mother?" the nurse asked.

My uncle pulled out his cell phone.

"Hey Sis. I'm at the hospital. Admire is awake. Get here as soon as you can." He had to leave a message.

My family was happy that I was out of the coma. That was the good news. The less pleasant news was the fact I was paralyzed from the waist down.

I tried not to cry, especially in front of my family. I had asked God not to let me die. And, he didn't. I had asked God to let me be fine. And, he did. But, he didn't make me just as I was before the accident. I hadn't thought to pray specifically for that, and now, I couldn't walk.

The doctor's said with physical therapy, my condition could change. I was determined to make that happen. I didn't want to go around for the rest of my life in a wheel chair. I couldn't imagine having to have people help me in and out of bed. I couldn't imagine not being able to run, jump, walk, or cheer anymore.

I was released from the hospital three days after I came out of the coma. My friends from school came to visit. Lucky for me, my accident happened the week before Christmas break. So, I hadn't missed much school. I never missed school because I didn't want to have to make up the work.

Christmas was going to be rough this year.

My family was happy I was home, but I knew they were sad I couldn't walk. Their prayers increased, but now included the phrase, "and Lord, please let Admire walk again."

SERENITY

I had a hard time trying to decide if I was going to apply for the L.M. Wilson Scholarship. My counselor at school gave me the flyer.

"Serenity, I believe you have a great opportunity here. This is a scholarship tailored for you. You just have to write an essay." My counselor was so bubbly and bossy. Sometimes she got on my nerves.

"Mrs. Pinbrook, I haven't decided I want to go to college right now. I have been struggling to get through this school year. I may just take a year off after high school, and work a little bit. I can always go to college later."

"Serenity, you are an honor student. The things you've been through these past few years are enough to break anybody, but you've managed to keep your head up, and persevere." She took a sip of her coffee.

I still wasn't sure, but to keep Mrs. Pinbrook from going on and on, I took the flyer and left her office.

I shoved it in my backpack as I headed to lunch.

That afternoon, as I sat in my room, I took the flyer out of my backpack. It was almost hopeless. College wasn't something my parents could afford. Especially after all the financial problems we'd been having the past two years.

My Aunt Sheryl and Uncle Thomas adopted me when I was born. My biological mother had gotten pregnant with me when she was sixteen. She was too young to take care of me, and she hadn't finished high school yet. Sheryl is my biological mom's sister, who is five years older than her.

She and her husband never had children of their own, but they spoiled me and always showered me with love.

My biological mom graduated from high school, but ended up meeting Mr. Wrong for her, who introduced her to drugs. She's been addicted to crack for years, and my family has had to use tough love when it comes to her.

Aunt Sheryl is a policewoman, and my uncle is a loan officer at a bank. Two years ago, Aunt Sheryl found out she had breast cancer, and our family has been struggling financially since then, because of the doctor bills.

"Serenity, what's wrong? When you came in the house, you came straight to your room. Did something happen at school today?" my aunt asked, as she brought me the mail that came for me that day.

Today must have been a good day for her. She was wearing her good wig, the one that my uncle liked. He said it reminded him of how she looked when they started dating in high school.

"I got this flyer today from Mrs. Pinbrook, the counselor at school. It's for a scholarship. But, I don't know if I really want to go to college next year."

"What do you mean? You don't know if you want to go to college? Ever since you were little, you've been making plans. You knew what kind of car you would drive, what kind of house you would live in, and how many children you would have. The last time I checked, you said you wanted to be a doctor."

"I know Auntie. But, things have changed over the past year. I know how long it's going to take for me to finish college if I want to become a doctor. Right now, I don't think I have the patience to go to school that long. I'm tired of school. So, maybe I will get a degree in Journalism. I would love to write for newspapers and magazines someday." I was flipping through the magazine she handed me, as I lay across my bed.

"Lord knows you've read plenty of magazines and books. You started reading when you were three, and that's been your favorite thing to do. So, fill out the application and see what happens. You never know what God has in store for you." My aunt smiled at me as she left my room.

I looked at the flyer again. "Who knows, maybe I will get it. If all I have to do is write an essay about myself and prove my birthday, how hard can it be?"

I got up from my bed and went into the living room. As I sat down in front of the computer, my mind became cloudy. I had no idea what to write about. As I sighed to myself, I began to type what came from my mind.

Dear Sir or Madam:

My name is Serenity Mechelle Bell. I was born March 2, 1989. I am seventeen years old and an honor student. I am in the band, on the student council, Editor for my school newspaper, on the Yearbook Committee and a volunteer at the hospital in the children's ward.

I could really use this scholarship because my family has been going through some tough times the past few years, and college isn't something we can afford to pay for.

My mom, who is really my aunt, has been fighting breast cancer, so our financial situation isn't the best at this time. My dad, who is really my uncle, works hard to make ends meet, but I don't think that college expenses are something that he can add to his plate right now.

When I was growing up, I loved to read. I would read any book about any subject. When my aunt became sick, I thought I wanted to become a doctor so that I could help find a cure for cancer. However, recently, I have changed my mind, and decided to pursue a degree in Journalism, because I love to write.

My life story isn't a fairy tale. My biological mother got pregnant with me when she was sixteen. She is very much a part of my life because my aunt and uncle wanted me to know her and love her, even if she wasn't able to take care of me. She is currently battling an addiction to drugs. I'm not ashamed to share that with others because my aunt and uncle have always said that the truth will make us free. Many people my age wouldn't admit they have a parent who is an addict. But her addiction isn't mine, her battle isn't mine, and I pray everyday she will get the help she needs.

I get teased a lot by my family and friends because of my love for Double Stuff Oreo Cookies. They tease me because of the way I eat them, the inside first, and then the outside. I also have a love for Cookies and Cream Ice Cream, and Cool Ranch Doritos. I eat Doritios every day.

I mentioned before that I love to read. I have so many books in my room, that I can start my own library. I love to read fiction books, and history books. Sometimes, I read books so fast my aunt encourages me to read them again to be sure I got the point.

I go to church every Sunday, although I will admit I don't always pay attention to what the preacher is saying. I sing in the choir, and the music is my favorite part of the service.

I hope you don't find my essay too personal, but I've always written from the heart.

In case you are wondering about my name, Serenity, it comes from the Serenity Prayer my grandma has prayed all of her life; God grant me the serenity to accept the things I cannot change, the courage to change the things I can, and the wisdom to know the difference. Simply stated, serenity means peace.

If you should find it in your heart to award me the L.M. Wilson Achievers Scholarship, my family and I would be very grateful.

I must have reread my essay twenty times. I wondered if I should have left the personal stuff out. But, I felt I should just be as honest as possible. I didn't want them to feel sorry for me, but I didn't want them to think my life was a fairy tale.

The next thing I had to do was find a photo to send with my essay.

I really didn't like taking pictures, although my friends always told me how pretty I was.

I went into my room, and looked in my keepsake box to see if there was a photo in it I wanted to send with my essay. None of them set right with my spirit. I grabbed my camera, as I looked at the clock. I was running out of time. I had to get the essay in the mail today, or I wouldn't make the deadline.

As I went through my digital camera, I ran across a photo my uncle had taken of my cousin Everett and I at a family reunion. People always said we looked enough alike to be brother and sister.

I printed the photo out, and hurriedly slipped it into the envelope. I ran into my aunt's room to grab a stamp off the dresser.

"Auntie, can you drive me to the post office please? I have to mail this today." She was in the middle of preparing dinner.

"Take my keys, and be careful Serenity. Pay attention to what you are doing. Don't mess with the radio, and don't show off for your friends. Don't speed and don't stop along the way. Go straight to the post office, and back," she said with a stern warning attached. "And remember, a car is not..."

"A toy, I know Auntie." I could finish her sentence for her because I had heard this speech a thousand times since I started driving.

"And don't forget to put your seat belt on!" She yelled as I ran out of the house.

As I drove to the post office, which was twenty minutes away from my house, I wondered if I should have chosen a different photo. Maybe I should have cropped my cousin Everett out of the photo, but it would have looked strange. I guess if I had just sent in a headshot, that would have sufficed, but as I looked at the clock, it was too late to go back home and change the photo. I hoped the scholarship committee wouldn't disqualify me for my choice. I should have thought about it before. It was too late now.

As I pulled up to the post office and placed my envelope in the mailbox, I heard sirens coming down the street. Auntie always told me to watch what I was doing and don't be nosing in other people's business, but I was curious to see where the sirens were headed. Something serious must have been going on.

I drove down the street, towards the direction of the sirens. As I approached the intersection, I saw a girl from my school pulling another girl out of a car. Then the car caught on fire.

MAMA

I was still mourning the loss of my son. It was Christmas Day, and I wouldn't get to hear his laugh, or see him sitting at the dinner table. My sister and her husband were there, Martin and Simone, my husband's brother and his wife, and my best friend Faye.

As glad as I was to have company, I was equally anxious for them to all leave so Martin and I could look at the envelopes he brought with him.

Laramie's girlfriend, Teresa called to wish me a Merry Christmas. I hadn't heard from her since the funeral. She sounded sad, and said she really missed my son. I told her to come visit me sometime because we were still her family. She promised she would visit the next time she was in town.

After the last piece of pecan pie was eaten, and the turkey and dressing had been placed in storage containers, the potato salad placed in the refrigerator, and the green bean casserole dish sat soaking in the sink, Martin and I walked our company to their cars.

Simone needed to go spend time with her family, so Martin and I would finally have the opportunity to read the essays and look through the photos.

I was nervous, but I prayed to God these envelopes indeed held the information about my grandchildren.

"Martin, I'm going to fix some coffee. You want some cake?" I asked him as I wiped the kitchen counter off.

"That Sock-it-to-Me Cake was delicious Mama. I could use another piece with my coffee. We only got three responses to the information I sent out. So hopefully these are the right three." He pulled the envelopes out of his briefcase and laid them on the table.

I had finished making coffee and had placed a nice sized piece of cake on a saucer in front of him. Then I sat down at the table, in a chair next to my son.

"Well, Mama. Which one do you want to open first?"

"It doesn't matter. Let's just get to it. I have butterflies in my stomach." I reached for one of the envelopes. It had pretty penmanship. Every letter was perfectly written in cursive.

I opened the envelope, and pulled out a photo of a beautiful caramel colored girl with beautiful brown eyes, defined cheekbones and shoulder length hair smiling at me. Immediately, I saw the resemblance. She didn't just resemble Laramie. She looked like I did when I was a teenager. This was the girl I saw that day I sat outside the school.

"I saw her," I said, pointing at the photo. "I knew the moment I laid eyes on her she was his daughter."

"When Mama? When did you see her?"

"A few weeks ago," I answered, after taking a sip of coffee. "I was having a bad day, and I drove to the high school. I just wanted to see if I could see him in any of those kids. And, then, this girl right here, walked out of the building and I knew she was my granddaughter. Look at her. Look at her eyes, and her cheek bones," I said, happy this one turned out to look like my son.

"I see a resemblance Mama." He grabbed the paperwork that was included in the envelope with the photo. He looked over the information sheet and then looked at a notepad he had written some notes on. "Well, the name listed on this application for her mother matches one of the names the private investigator gave me."

"This girl's name is Myracle Michelle Lee. Here's her essay Mama," he said, as he handed it to me.

I handed it back to him. "You read it to me," I said. I wanted to just soak in every word he read from the paper while I stared at the photo of my son's beautiful daughter. As I listened to her thoughts, through Martin's voice, I was glad to hear she was well taken care of and she loved to read. I was happy God had been introduced to her and proud she planned to go to college.

"Read it again, Martin. Please?" I asked. I wanted to hear about her again.

After he finished reading Myracle's essay, he placed it on top of the envelope it came in, and slid it to the middle of the table.

He picked up the next envelope. As he opened it, I placed Myracle's photo on top of her essay.

He opened the envelope, and pulled out the paperwork. I reached for the photo which had been paper clipped to the top sheet.

I saw dancing eyes within the beautiful face of a mocha colored cheerleader with a smile I had seen before. It was Laramie's smile. Those eyes were his too. She was definitely his little girl. I grabbed the photo of the first girl, and placed the two side by side. The two girls were definitely sisters. I wondered how they attended the same school, but no one had realized they were related.

"This one's name is Admire Mychel Johnson. That's different. The name on her application matches the other name I have." He read the essay aloud as I stared at the photos of my grandchildren.

Then, the last envelope was opened. Martin hadn't been able to locate the third girl Laramie had told her about, so he didn't know if they would be disappointed.

As soon as he pulled her photo out of the envelope, and handed it to me, I could see that this butterscotch colored girl was also my son's child, but I was confused because there was a young man in the photo with her who also looked like my son. He too was the color of butterscotch.

"What's her name?" I asked. I placed the photo next to the others. There was no mistake these were my son's daughters. And the young man was probably, his son too.

"Her name is Serenity Mechelle Bell." He read her essay to me. I cried. "There's no mention of who the young man is in the photo?" I asked.

"No Mama. But they look familiar to me. I've seen these kids before."

"Where did you see them? Did you think when you saw them that they looked like your brother?"

"I don't recall Mama. I just know I've seen these kids before. It will come back to me. This is interesting information. She was adopted by her aunt, her mother's sister. It's so sad that her mother is on drugs." My son had taken his last bite of cake.

I couldn't stop looking at the photos of the kids. Something was strange about Serenity's photo.

"Martin, all four of these young people are our family. We need to find out who this young man is in the photo. Evidently your brother had another child he didn't know about. All the birthdays match up, which is so odd. How in the world did three young women, who happen to be pregnant by the same man, happen to have their babies on the same day?" I asked aloud, not expecting an answer.

"I don't know Mama. But here's proof it happened. Do you think we should get DNA tests to be sure they are his?"

"We can, just to be safe. But I know in my heart these are Laramie's children. I can go pull out photos from years ago and you will see our family genes in these children. And that boy, he looks like Laramie did when he was in the tenth grade." I got up from the table and went into the living room to get a photo album of the kid's school pictures. After flipping through it for a few minutes, I found the photo of Laramie that resembled the boy in the photo with Serenity.

"He does look like Laramie, Mama. I guess we will find out more when we set up a time to meet them."

"Yes. I guess so. We need to do it, sooner than later. I don't want to wait until March to meet my grandchildren. We need to do it sooner. The other thing which is odd to me is they all have the same middle name, just spelled different. My goodness."

I took an ink pen, and wrote the girl's names on the back of their photos, then placed them back on the table on top of their essays.

That night, after Martin had gone home, and I was alone, I found myself at the kitchen table looking at the photos of the children.

I reread each essay, and said a silent prayer for each of them.

A few days after Christmas, I was gathering up newspapers and mail I had allowed to pile up. I skimmed through a few pages of the newspaper, just to make sure I hadn't missed any important news.

As I got ready to put the last paper in the recycle box, a story about a teenage girl in a fiery car crash caught my eye. How terrible I thought. I took a moment to read the story that accompanied the photo of the burning car that had been struck by an eighteen-wheeler.

> "A seventeen-year-old local high school student was taken to the hospital after an eighteen-wheeler collided with the blue Toyota Corolla she was driving.
>
> The student, Admire Johnson, was unconscious at the scene and was pulled from the car by another high school student, Myracle Lee, just before the car caught

on fire. Johnson is listed in critical condition at County Hospital."

I could hardly catch my breath. I looked to see what date was on the paper. December 15. I didn't recall reading the newspaper that day, or hearing about the story. But even if I had, would it have caught my attention? Seventeen days before this moment, I wouldn't have recognized their names…I wouldn't have known they were my grandchildren.

I picked up the phone to call Martin.

"Hello," he said.

"Martin, this is your mother." I was starting to have chest pains. Something I hadn't had in years.

"Yes Mama, I recognize your voice. How are you this morning…at, ummm, 7:30 a.m.?"

"I'm not so good at the moment. I'm having chest pains, but that's not why I called you…" I was trying to continue, but Martin interrupted me.

"Chest pains! Mama, I'm calling 911. You need to get to the hospital!"

"Son, I will be fine, don't waste your time calling 911. I'm just a little shaken this morning. Are you on your way to work?" I asked, walking towards the refrigerator to get a bottle of water.

"I'm leaving in a few minutes, but from the sound of things, I need to come by and see you before I go to work."

"Yes, Son, I think that would be a good idea. I need to show you something." I didn't wait to say goodbye. I hung the phone up and sat at the kitchen table with the newspaper, the essays and the photos of my grandchildren.

MARTIN

Something had been bothering me since the night we looked at the photos of the kids. I had seen that photo of Serenity and the unnamed young man before. I just couldn't remember where.

I was glad the pieces to the seventeen-year-old puzzle seemed to be coming together. I could tell mama was relieved we had found children who looked as if they were Laramie's. All we had to do now was get solid proof, by getting them to take a DNA test. I believed the test was more important now, since there was the possibility the young man in the photo was my nephew.

As I was getting ready for work one morning, a few days after Christmas, mama called me and said she needed to show me something. There was a sense of urgency in her voice, so I knew it must be important.

It was cold that morning, and the weatherman said there was a chance for freezing rain and snow headed our direction. I wasn't looking forward to bad weather. There were so many people who didn't drive well in icy conditions, and I didn't like having to worry about if some haphazard driver would hit my car.

As I drove to mama's house that morning, the song *Unpredictable* by Jamie Foxx and Ludacris was on the radio. Unpredictable was a great word to describe how the situation we were dealing with could end up. Who knew if the people who had been taking care of these children for seventeen years would be receptive to us?

Snow flurries had started to fall on my windshield as I pulled in to mama's driveway. I could see her through the living room window sitting at the table, with both hands folded across her chest. I didn't like what her body language was saying at that moment.

"Hey Mama, did you make coffee this morning?" I asked, as I took off my coat and gloves and laid them in a chair in the kitchen. I headed towards the pantry.

"I made some earlier, but we should probably put on another pot," she said, as she walked over to the cabinet where she kept the coffee.

"I'm starving. You have any Malt-o-Meal? You know I need something to warm me up on the inside." I found the Malt-O-Meal in the cabinet, and got a pot out so I could make some breakfast. "You want some Mama?"

"No, Baby. I don't have much of an appetite this morning."

"It's beginning to snow out there. I may not even go into the office today. I think I'm going to hang out here with you today, and let those crazy drivers have at it."

Mama was rather quiet as I ate my breakfast. The small television in the kitchen was on one of those Court TV shows. After I finished and cleaned up the mess I'd made, mama told me to come sit at the table with her.

She slid a newspaper towards me. I picked it up, not realizing what relevance it had.

"What is this Mama?" I asked, trying to figure out what she was showing me.

She pointed at a photo of a car on fire.

"Read the story," she said, as her voice trailed off. She coughed, as if she were getting strangled. I was about to get up to get her a glass of water, but she patted me on my shoulder and motioned for me to sit down.

I picked up the newspaper and read the story. When I came across Admire and Myracle's names, I realized why my mother had lost her desire to eat.

"When did this happen?" I asked, looking for the date of the article.

"A few weeks before Christmas. I looked through the other papers I had to see if an update had been printed, but there wasn't anything. I looked in the obituaries too. She wasn't in there either."

"Well, that's a good sign. I'll call the hospital and see if she is still there," I said, getting up from the table to get the phone book.

"I'm going to trust God that she is fine. I think it's all a part of God's plan that one of Laramie's children saved the other one's life. It's nothing but God working through this situation." She got up, and walked over to pour herself a cup of coffee. I guess her appetite was coming back because she was cutting herself a slice of cake. "You want a piece?"

"Yes Ma'am. You know I love cake. Do you have some milk?" She nodded, as the lady on the phone begin to talk.

"Ok. Well, thank you for your help," I said, as I hung up the phone.

"Admire was released from the hospital a few days before Christmas," I said, taking a bite of cake.

"Well, praise God. I'm so glad she's fine," mama said, with a look of relief on her face.

"Fine may be stretching it. The lady I spoke with is one of Simone's friends. She said Admire is paralyzed from the waist down. They are hoping with therapy, she will regain activity in her legs."

Mama looked at me with tears in her eyes. "I guess we need to pray she walks again. She's so young. She's a cheerleader. I wonder how she's dealing with this. In her essay, she was so bubbly. I wonder if this will change her," mama said, taking a sip of her coffee. "I need to see her, Martin. I need to know how she's doing." Mama glared at the judge on television.

"Not yet Mama. I will try to find out how she is. We have to wait. If you want, we can move up the date to meet the girls." I walked over to my briefcase and pulled out my planner. As I sat back down and took a drink of milk, I found a date on my calendar that was open.

"Yes, I think we should move the date. I want to meet them in the next few weeks. All of this waiting is not easy for me. I'm getting too old for all of these surprises."

"Old? I have never heard you use the word old to describe yourself. How about I send out letters to meet with them the Saturday after MLK Day?"

"That will be fine. I think we should have them come here," mama said.

I didn't agree.

"Why Mama? I think we should meet them at my office first. It's a neutral place. What if these girls aren't trustworthy? We don't know them, only what they wrote in their essays. You live alone, so for right now, until we know how they will react to the news this scholarship is actually money their father, whom they've never met, left them, we should meet in a neutral place."

"I think your office is so, intimidating Martin. These girls are our family. I want them to feel comfortable and open to us. I want them to feel at home. Especially if Admire is in jeopardy of never being able to walk again, I want her to feel at home here." Mama gave me that look of hers which meant it wasn't up for discussion. But I was determined to stand my ground on this decision.

"How about, we compromise. We can meet the girls individually at my office, for a...pre-interview. We can get to know them, informally, and invite them to a more relaxed meeting here, where we can have a nice lunch or dinner with all of them. Then we can share with them what the scholarship is really about." I walked over to the window. The snow was beginning to fall faster. The hood of my car was covered.

Mama looked as if she was pondering my proposal. For a long time, she didn't say anything.

She got up from the table and went to the sink to wash her hands. She got a pot out from under the cabinet, and rinsed it out before setting it on the stove. She opened the package of meat that was in the sink and put it in the pot.

"It's a very cold day. It's a good day for chili. From the way it looks outside, I guess you'll be staying for dinner Martin." She began to put the seasonings and tomatoes in the pot.

"Yes Ma'am. I'm not in a hurry to slip and slide out there in that icy mess. I'm going to just spend the day with you, and maybe even beat you in a game of Scrabble." I knew that would get her to smile.

"Beat me? You have never beat me at Scrabble." She smiled as she placed the lid on the pot.

"Yes I did, once, a long time ago. But it seems you can't remember. Are you going to make some cornbread to go with that chili?" I asked.

"You have hands. You are more than welcome to make the cornbread." She laughed, something I hadn't heard her do since my brother died.

I went to my room down the hall to change out of my suit. I kept clothes at mama's house because I spent a lot of time there. I never wanted to be caught unprepared if mama needed me to do something that required me to get dirty. I definitely wasn't going to mow the lawn or look under the hood of mama's car in my nice suit.

Mama came to the door of my room as I was getting the Scrabble game out of my closet.

"Ok Martin," she said, quietly.

I turned to look at her. "Ok what Mama?"

"Ok. We will meet with the girls at your office first. Then, we will invite them here for dinner. I understand the need to be cautious right now. This is a sensitive situation, for everyone involved, but especially for the girls."

"I hear what you're saying Mama. I am hoping for the best, but I have to be prepared for small surprises." We went back into the kitchen and placed the Scrabble game on the table.

"How long before the chili is ready? I'm hungry. You have any snacks?" I ate more at mama's house than I did anywhere else. It was just something about mama's kitchen that made me hungry. I looked in the cabinet and found the tea bags.

"You need to measure that sugar before you pour it into the pitcher!" Mama always fussed at us about the amount of sugar we used when we made Kool-Aid and tea. We usually just poured the sugar in the container and continued to add more until we felt our concoction was sweet enough.

"I have been making tea for a long time Mama. L and I perfected this method of making Kool-Aid and tea a long time ago. See, to you it just looks like we don't measure the sugar. But when we were little, and daddy taught us how to make Kool-Aid, he marked this pitcher with a black line. He said if we poured the sugar in to right here," I held up the pitcher to show her the line that looked like a normal spot to the untrained eye, "then it would be sweet enough. Now, L always poured a little more because he liked his drinks a lot sweeter, but for the most part, this is the right amount." I smiled at her.

"Well, I guess that's another family secret. He used to drive me crazy pouring the sugar in without measuring it."

"He did it on purpose. He said he liked to hear you fuss about it because you were so cute when you fussed."

Mama blushed.

She beat me three to one in Scrabble that day. Her chili and my cornbread complimented each other quite well.

MYRACLE

Christmas was great that year. My whole family was at Grand D and Granny's house. We had a huge Christmas tree with many presents in the living room.

I loved Christmas. Next to my birthday, it was my favorite holiday. I didn't like it just because I got presents, I liked it because I saved my money all year and was able to buy everyone in my family a present, all thirty-seven of them. Granny had taught me how to shop for things on clearance and on sale, so I knew how to make my money stretch. Grand D gave me twenty dollars a week and I used some to pay for my lunch at school, but I saved most of it.

My family was really excited about me being in the newspaper for saving that girl's life from my school. It was no big deal to me. I just heard the crash that day as I was leaving the post office, and ran to see if anybody needed help. That girl from the cheerleading squad wasn't conscious, so when I saw the flames coming from the fuel tank area, I knew I had to pull her out of the car. I had second thoughts because I had been taught in First Aid and CPR training not to move injured patients. But this had to be an exception to the rule.

Just as I pulled her out of the car and managed to drag her to the sidewalk a few feet away, the car blew up. It was one of the scariest things I'd ever experienced in my life.

I checked for a pulse. She had one. Then, the fire trucks, ambulance and police all seemed to show up at the same time.

People called me a hero. Well, some called me a heroine. But I didn't see myself that way. I just helped somebody who needed help. I would like to believe if I were in a life and death situation, someone would help me.

My mother called me to tell me Admire's mother wanted to meet me so she could thank me for saving her daughter's life. I told her I would think about it and get back to her.

My mother didn't make it to Christmas dinner that year because she had to work at the hospital. She brought my Christmas present over the day before and put it under the tree so I could open it when I opened the other ones.

Our relationship wasn't the greatest. She rarely had time for me. She would take me out to dinner every once in awhile, and take me shopping, but we never talked about important stuff the way mothers and daughters are supposed to. I believe she was jealous with the relationship I had with my grandparents and my uncle. I loved her, regardless of what was missing in our relationship.

My family knew my favorite colors were pink and purple. So, because I was the only girl of all my cousins, I got a lot of cool stuff for Christmas. My room was decorated with pink and purple flowers and butterflies on the walls. My bedspread was purple and my accent pillows were pink.

That Christmas, I got something I wasn't expecting. As I unwrapped my packages with the pretty bows, there seemed to be a theme of some sort I didn't understand at first.

One box had an *India Arie* CD, another had a *Yolanda Adams* CD, and another had a *Beyonce* CD. One of the boxes had an emergency car kit in it, and another had a purple and pink butterfly keychain. Another one of the boxes, which was a little bigger than the others, had purple seat covers in it, but I didn't have a car. So, I started thinking as I continued to open my gifts. They all had something to do with a car! My favorite uncle's gift to me contained a car CD player, while my grandparent's gift to me was in a medium sized box. As I opened it, I didn't know what to expect.

I opened one box, and inside of it, was another box. I opened that box, and inside it was another box. Five boxes later, I opened the last box to find a note that said, "Go look in the driveway".

I ran to the back door with the biggest grin on my face. My uncle was right behind me. Grand D had already managed to get outside before I opened the door to find a Volkswagen Bug sitting in the driveway.

It wasn't a new one. It was the old one that I had passed by everyday on my way to school and had claimed as my car. A few weeks ago, when I passed by the car lot on my way home from school, I noticed it was gone.

My grandparents had bought it for me, and my Uncle Terry had it painted pink with a purple butterfly on the hood. It also had purple pin stripes down the sides. It was the coolest thing I had ever seen. And it was just for me.

I screamed when I saw it. I hugged everybody, but I hugged Grand D and Uncle Terry the hardest.

"I guess that means you like it?" Granny said, as she stood outside shivering in the cold air.

"I love it! This is the best Christmas ever!" I said as I kissed her on the cheek. I ran over to the car and opened the door. I sat down inside, and noticed the interior was shiny and the rugs were clean. It smelled like Vanilla, which was my favorite smell.

"Do you want to drive it?" Uncle Terry asked, dangling the keys in my face, as he got in on the passenger side.

"Of course I do!" I said, as we shut the doors. I started up the car, put my seat belt on and then I adjusted my seat and rear view mirrors, as I started to back out of the driveway. "My own car! I can't believe it," I said, smiling at my uncle.

After we drove around for thirty minutes, we headed back to the house for dinner. I was starving too. I loved Christmas dinner. Turkey and dressing, potato salad, broccoli and rice casserole were all I needed. My favorite desert was triple chocolate cake with Cookies and Cream Ice Cream.

I had managed to earn a seat at the grown up table this year because my mother wasn't there for dinner. I was glad too because my cousins were so gross sometimes. They burped and passed gas at the table. They were totally disgusting.

The topic of conversation that day happened to be me, and all the things my family had been hearing about me since my name was mentioned in the newspaper.

"I heard you might get an award from the mayor. They have a ceremony each year for people who have helped save someone's life. My cousin works at the mayor's office, and she mentioned your name." Aunt

Denise said. She was my uncle Jerry's wife. Uncle Jerry was my mom's oldest brother.

"Oh, how exciting," Granny said, with a big smile. "I'm going to have to buy me a new dress for that."

Uncle Henry was sitting next to her and managed to speak, between bites of turkey and cranberry sauce. "I heard the Elks Lodge president was so impressed, they want to present Myracle with a Scholarship for college. He said it's something they do to reward young people in the community for their leadership efforts and commitment to the community."

Grand D was sitting at the head of the table. His chest was sticking out, as if he was the proudest man alive.

"I'm proud of our little Myracle. I know she didn't do what she did for all of this. But, God blesses people when they are a blessing to others." He took a sip of his tea, and reached over to touch Granny's hand.

There were still more presents under the tree that I hadn't opened. I had gotten so excited about the car I left my other presents unattended. My cousins were trying to open them for me, but that was not going to happen.

I waited until later that night to open up the rest of my gifts. My attention had fallen to the telephone that began to ring. One friend after the other called to talk about their gifts. They were excited to hear about my car, as I was the only one of us who got one.

After my last phone call ended around 8:30 that night, our other family members had begun to leave. I helped clean up the kitchen then I went into the living room and sat down on the floor in front of the Christmas tree. Granny came in and sat down on the sofa.

I opened up one present that was from granny's sister. It was a pair of pink gloves. Another box had a purse I'd wanted. It was from granny. Then, I came to a box that had my mother's handwriting on it. It was small, so I knew before I opened it that jewelry was inside.

"Oh, that's pretty," granny said, as I held up the gold charm bracelet. It had seventeen charms on it, each representing a different stage in my life. One charm was of a book, another of a bicycle, one of a skate, and so on.

There was another box in the shape of a book, but when I tore the wrapping paper off, it was a picture frame with a note attached to it. The note stated,

"Myracle,

All little girls should know who their dad is. This is the only picture I have of yours. So many times you've asked me questions about him. I took the time to jot down everything I remembered about him on the back of his photo. I hope this answers some of your questions.

I'm proud of the young woman you have become. Maybe one day, things will get better between us.

Merry Christmas.
Love,
Your Mother"

This photo was definitely a surprise. My mother had never said much about my father. I thought she must have hated him because of the way she responded when I brought him up.

I examined the picture of the man in the frame. I saw the same eyes in the photo I saw every morning when I looked in the mirror at myself. His lips and his nose were the same as mine too. The only thing I got from my mother was her color. His eyes were the same shade of brown as mine. It was unbelievable how much I looked like him.

Grand D came into the living room and sat down in his favorite chair.

"What you got there, little girl?" he said.

"It's a gift from my mother Grand D. A picture of my...father," I answered.

"Let me see?" he said, as he stretched out his hand towards me.

I handed him the picture, as I moved over towards his chair.

"That's an interesting gift your mother chose to give you for Christmas," Granny said.

"I'd have to agree with you on that Honey. Nice picture. You look like him," Grand D commented.

"Did either of you ever meet him?" I enquired, as he handed the picture back to me.

"Yes, we met him. Your mother wasn't allowed to date anyone that we didn't meet first. He came to the house a few times. As I recall, he was a nice young fellow, smart, intelligent, nice manners. Your mother was crazy about him," Granny answered. She was working on a crossword puzzle, and had gotten stuck. "What's the name of that singing group with those three girls? Somebody's child…"

I laughed. "Destiny's Child Granny. How long did they date?"

"I don't know Myracle. I guess a few months. He was a football player, if I recall correctly. Your mother thought she was in love. Then, she found out she was pregnant after he had gone away to college. And when she told him, he must not have reacted the way she hoped because she didn't talk about him anymore, and didn't want us to mention his name," Grand D added. "I think I need a piece of that sweet potato pie in the kitchen. It's calling my name. Didn't y'all hear it?" He laughed as he looked at Granny and me.

I laughed at him. "No, I didn't hear it, but I will get you a piece." I got up from the floor and headed to the kitchen.

I could hear my grandparents talking in the other room.

"I wonder what's going on in Alicia's mind, giving Myracle that picture. I think that maybe she should have just talked to her about it, instead of wrapping it up for a present and leaving it under the tree," Granny said, with a tone of disappointment.

"I don't know. But Myracle has always wanted to know about him. So, as long as that baby girl in there is happy, that's all that matters to me. I don't think this will take away her joy. So, let's just see where this goes," Grand D said, as I entered the room with a nice sized slice of pie on a saucer and a tall glass of milk.

"You are going to be sick tonight, Donald!" Granny scolded.

"I will be just fine. It's the holidays, so I can afford to splurge a little," Grand D said, as he took a bite of his pie, and wiggled his toes at the same time. Grand D always said when something tasted good it made his toes wiggle.

"Well, I am going to turn in for the night. Thank you for a great Christmas. I love my car, and I promise to be responsible." I kissed Granny good night first, then Grand D.

"Good night Sugar. Sleep tight. Don't forget to say your prayers," Granny reminded me, just as she had every night since I learned to talk.

"I won't Granny."

"Don't let the bedbugs bite," Grand D called after me.

I turned and smiled at him, as I picked my things up from the living room floor and headed down the hallway.

After I closed the door to my bedroom, I sat on my bed and stared at the picture of my father. I wondered what it would have been like to talk to him. I turned the picture over, and looked at the notes my mother had written on the back.

> Laramie Mitchell
> Honor student
> Star athlete
> Intelligent
> Goals in life are to play pro-football and coach
> Fav. color is blue
> Fav. movies: Coming to America and Die Hard
> Fav. singers: Michael Jackson and Janet Jackson
> Fav. food: Pizza, Double Stuff Oreos and Cool Ranch Doritos
> Weird thing about him is he ate ketchup on almost everything and ate Cookies and Cream Ice Cream everyday
> He believed in God.

I turned the picture back over and looked at it.

I sighed as I placed it on the desk next to the picture of my best friends.

I had a hard time sleeping that night. The car, all the excitement of Christmas day, and the picture of my father were hindering to my sleep.

ADMIRE

Christmas was hard that year on my family. No one wanted to focus on my current disability. Everyone tried to act as if things were normal. But they weren't.

I was beginning to slip into depression. I couldn't believe I couldn't walk or move my legs. I was a pretty independent person, and my current circumstance made me dependent on my family.

I prayed to God several times a day. I prayed for the ability to understand why this had happened to me. I prayed for the patience I needed until God gave me back the activity of my legs. I prayed for determination to push myself, no matter how hard physical therapy was. I prayed for continuous faith the size of a mustard seed that I heard the preacher talk about at church.

I wanted to walk, run, turn cartwheels, dance and be my normal self.

My mother told me I had to take charge of my circumstance instead of allowing my circumstance to take charge of me. I heard what she was saying, but it was a easier said than done.

For as long as I could remember, I had helped my mother cook Christmas dinner. When I woke up that Christmas morning, I decided this Christmas would be no different. Family was coming to spend the day with us, and I was going to do my best to be my usually cheerful and upbeat self.

I began my day by getting out of bed without help and easing into the wheelchair beside my bed. It took about fifteen minutes and I was tired after I had completed my task. I sat there for a few minutes and looked around my bedroom. The bright orange, yellow and pink colors scattered throughout, normally made me feel inspired. Not that day. When my eyes caught a glimpse of the photo on my dresser of my cheerleading squad, I became teary eyed. I wanted more than anything to cheer again. We had several competitions coming up in the spring, and my squad had been National Cheerleading Champions twice since I became a cheerleader. This was my senior year, and I wanted to leave my mark on the school in a big way. I didn't want to be remembered as the cheerleader who had a car wreck her senior year, and became paralyzed.

My stepfather knocked on my door as I was rolling towards it.

"Come in," I said.

"You're up I see. I was coming to get you because the boys were waiting to open up the Christmas presents," he said, as he stood in the doorway. "I see you didn't need my help this morning. I guess you're getting your strength back." He smiled at me.

"I want things to get back to normal. I was going to help Mama in the kitchen after I took a shower and dressed myself." I rolled myself towards the dresser to get some clothes out.

"Ok. Well let me get your mother so she can help you into the shower," he said, as he turned to walk down the hallway towards the kitchen.

"No, don't get her. I want to try to do it myself. If I need help, I'll call her." There was a look of surprise on his face.

"Well, alright then, Miss Independent. I'm glad to see you're back to your old self."

"I'm trying. This thing with people waiting on me and carrying me just isn't normal. I didn't like to be carried around when I was little, so I learned to walk at eight months, or at least that's what my family has always told me. So, I would like to see how much I can do by myself," I managed a smile, as I rolled towards the door, and headed to the bathroom down the hall.

It wasn't easy getting into the bathtub by myself. I fell the first time I tried to transition from my wheelchair into the bathtub. I hit my head on the side of the tub. It must have made a loud noise, because I heard my mother at the door.

"Admire, are you alright?" she asked while trying to open the door.

"I'm okay, Mama. I fell, but I'm okay," I answered while trying to get up off the floor. It took awhile, but I managed to get into the tub, out of the tub, and dress myself.

When I opened up the bathroom door, my mother was standing in the hallway with a worried look on her face. "You okay," she asked, staring at the knot that was forming on my forehead.

"Yes, Ma'am. I'm okay. I wanted to do it by myself."

"Okay then. Come on, the boys are waiting for you to open up presents. And you need to put some ice on that knot before it gets bigger." She couldn't resist the need to push my wheelchair down the hallway. I didn't say anything because I was tired after using my muscles to get in and out of the tub. I was happy to know I could do it by myself. To me, it was a positive sign I was on my way back to living a normal life. Well, as much as normal could be, given my current situation.

That Christmas I got a new cell phone, something I had been asking for all year. I also got clothes and shoes, and my class ring. It was a great Christmas.

My job in the kitchen was desserts. I loved baking cookies and my family enjoyed eating them just as much as I enjoyed making them. It was kind of hard maneuvering my way around the kitchen because the counter top was much higher than the wheel chair would allow me to reach. My mom suggested I use the kitchen table to mix my cookies, and accept the help offered to me by my family to put them in the oven.

"They are still your cookies, Admire. You just need a little help putting them in the oven. You tell us when, and we'll take them out for you." My mother knew how much I wanted to be able to do things on my own. I loved her for understanding, and I loved my family for not making me feel helpless.

Some of my friends stopped by to bring me gifts and we hung out in my room and for a while, everything seemed normal, the way it was before the accident. I sat on my bed, and my friends, Lisa and Kim were stretched out on the floor. We listened to music, and they helped me set up my new phone. We ate cookies, and talked about the latest high school gossip.

Kim and I had been friends since elementary school. She was a cheerleader too. Lisa was also a cheerleader and had only been a student at our school for two years. They were my closest friends. My mother always said we need at least two good friends, one to make us laugh, and the other to keep us grounded. I believe my two friends had that covered.

"So, I heard Myracle Lee saved your life?" Kim said. She was flipping through a magazine trying to find a new style to try on her wavy hair that cascaded down her back.

"Yes, that's what my mom told me. I can't wait to get back to school so I can thank her in person. I guess if she hadn't been there, I wouldn't be here," I answered, trying to readjust myself on the bed.

Lisa looked at me. She was the one who kept me grounded. "I still think it's so weird how much the two of you look alike."

"I don't think we look that much alike Lisa. But, as they say, everybody has a twin somewhere."

"I have to agree with Lisa. Admire, you just can't see it. But if the two of you were standing in the mirror in the same room, at the same time, you'd see it. I was walking down the hallway one day, and I thought she was you. The only difference is the way you wear your hair. Hers is shoulder length, but you keep yours in a bob."

Lisa got up from the floor and walked over to my bookshelf. She grabbed my yearbook from my junior year and started turning the pages. When she got to what she was looking for, she sat down on my bed beside me, and handed the book to me.

"Look at her." She was pointing to a picture of Myracle.

"She's cute," I said, looking at the picture and not really noticing any resemblance.

Lisa got up from my bed and grabbed a small picture of me that was stuck to the mirror of my dresser. She placed my picture next to Myracle's picture, and looked at me.

"Do you see it now?" she asked, determined to make me see her point.

"Let me see," said Kim, as she came and sat on the other side of me, so that I was sandwiched between my two best friends. She examined the two pictures, and looked at me. "See, you two have the same eyes, the same nose, and almost the same smile. She could easily pass for your sister," she said.

"I guess," I replied, as I began to see what my friends were showing me. "Well, I guess she's my look-a-like then," I commented with a laugh.

"Yeah, I would say so," Kim said. We looked through the yearbook for a while, and then Kim said, "She looks like you too," as she pointed to the picture of a girl who was on the Yearbook committee. "I heard she was really smart too."

"Okay, could you two please stop trying to find everybody that you think looks like me? Fortunately, for all of us, there is only one Admire Mychel Johnson. I am an original, not a carbon copy."

My friends laughed at me.

"Have you heard from Austin?" Kim asked. Austin was my boyfriend.

"No, he hasn't called me. I tried calling him, but he didn't answer. So, you know me, I am not about to keep calling him. I don't want it to seem like I'm chasing him. I guess he's turned off by the fact I can't walk now. So, if that's the case, then I don't need him," I responded.

"I agree. I never really liked him anyway," Lisa replied. "I don't think he was on your level. And seeing as how your mother didn't really care for him, it is probably best that things aren't going to work out."

"Whatever," Kim said. "He still could have called or sent flowers or something. I think he's a coward to dump somebody without telling them."

"I'm not even upset. I'm kind of glad it happened this way. He had started trying to pressure me into having sex, and I'm not ready for that. My mom would kill me if she found out I had been sneaking out to be with him, and she would bring me back from the dead and kill me again if she thought I was having sex."

"I heard he used to hit his previous girlfriend," Lisa said.

"What do you mean by hit?" I asked, shocked by her statement.

"Like, slap her! Punch her! Hit!" Lisa said, using her hands to make the point more clear.

"Did he ever hit you Admire?" Kim asked.

I looked at her and laughed. "Me? Heck no! You know I don't play that. My uncle and my mom told me I was special and that if a guy ever tried to put his hands on me, he didn't love me or care about me. My uncle told me to let him know if it ever happened, and he would cut off the hand the guy used to hit me with."

Lisa and Kim laughed.

"You know, some girls think it's okay for their boyfriends to hit them. My cousin Leslie used to date this guy who hit her and left bruises all the time. She said she loved him, and understood he was going through something. But the last time he hit her he broke three of her ribs. That's when my uncle found out what had been going on and made her press charges against him."

"I don't know why any girl or woman would think it's okay for someone to hit them. I love myself too much to let that happen," Kim replied.

"Me too," I added.

That night, after my company had gone home, and it was just my family, my mom came into my room with a gift I had forgotten to open.

"Who is it from?" I asked, tearing off the bow, and wrapping paper.

"From me," she said, smiling as she watched me open the box.

It was a necklace with an amethyst stone pendant, something I had been wanting for a long time.

I hugged her tightly for a few minutes.

"Thanks Mom. I really love it!" I said, as she helped me put it on.

"You're welcome Admire. I know the past few weeks have been hard on you. I saw you last week getting frustrated because you had to rely on us to help you move around. You have always been a determined little girl, so I have no doubt you will get through this time in your life. My daddy used to say tough times don't last, tough people do. You are a tough young lady, and I know you are already trying to figure out how you are going to stand at the podium to give your valedictorian speech on graduation day. But, even if it isn't part of God's plan for you to walk again, and I have been praying that this isn't the case, you are still a beautiful, smart and intelligent young woman who will give that speech no matter what." My mom had tears in her eyes.

She hugged me again then got up to leave my room. She stopped by the open yearbook lying on my desk. She looked at it for a few minutes and said, "Myracle Lee. That's a nice picture of her. Do you have any classes together?"

"No. We did last year. Kim and Lisa think we look alike."

My mom looked at the picture again and then at me. "I can see the resemblance. But, then again, everybody looks like somebody," she said, as she picked up the empty plate which once held my famous chocolate chip cookies, and headed for the door. "Do you want me to help you get ready for bed?"

"No thanks. I believe I can do it by myself."

"Well, if you need anything, just let me know."

I couldn't sleep that night, so I sat up in my bed and finished reading the James Patterson book I'd started before my accident. I tried to start the new John Grisham book my Uncle Vincent bought me, but my mind started wandering.

I tried to tell myself I wasn't upset I hadn't heard from my boyfriend since my accident. I really liked him. He was smart and really cute. It was hard to believe he hit on his former girlfriend. I don't know what I would have done if he had hit me. I definitely don't think I would have kept seeing him.

My uncle Vincent thought he wasn't good enough for me. Maybe he was right.

SERENITY

I have never been a big fan of Christmas. The holidays were usually when my family all got together at my Nana's house. There were a lot of us, and we stayed all day. So I always took a couple of books with me to keep me occupied. I hid in my grandmother's room and tried to stay to myself. Some members of my family were annoying, and I wasn't much of a pro at hiding my facial expressions. My uncle always said people could read me like a book, so I had to try extra hard to hide what I was thinking.

My biological mother usually showed up to the family gathering. I hated seeing her wasting away, but Nana said as long as my mother showed up, the family knew she was alive.

Before we went to Nana's house, I helped Auntie bake a peach cobbler. I made Rice Krispy Treats for the kids who were going to be there, and I put a couple of pieces in my bag, along with my books just in case my cousins got greedy.

The only part about family gatherings I liked was seeing my cousin Everett. He was the same age as me, and we liked a lot of the same things. Reading was one of them.

Up until two years ago, Everett and I went to the same school. My Aunt Sarah got a new job in another state, so I only get to see him on holidays.

I prayed before getting to Nana's house my mother would have a good day, and not show up high. I always worried something bad would happen to her.

At Nana's house, I got a few gifts from family members: some socks, a gift card to my favorite book store, an *Alicia Keys* CD, some bangle bracelets and a couple of sweaters. Every year I got socks and bracelets from the same family members, so I knew before opening the package what was in there. I just didn't know what color it would be.

My Nana made the best dressing in the world, and my Uncle Paul made the best cabbage in the world. I didn't really care for turkey, and neither did my cousin Everett. For some reason, we both preferred chicken, so Nana always fixed some chicken for us.

My mother showed up after everyone had eaten dinner. I was in Nana's room when Everett came to tell me.

"Your mama's in there, and she doesn't look too good. She started hugging on me, and rubbing my face. I had to get out of there," he said. He came and sat down on the floor beside me. "What are you reading?"

"The Color Purple," I answered, while shoving a piece of Rice Krispy Treat in my mouth.

"You must have snuck that piece away before the other kids got to it," he said, smiling as he picked up the other book I had brought with me.

"James Patterson, I like his books. I haven't read this one yet," he said, skimming the back cover.

I handed him a Rice Krispy Treat. "Thanks Cuz," he said, as he opened the book he'd brought with him.

"What are you reading?" I asked.

"*Standing at the Scratch Line.*"

"I haven't heard of that book before. Who is the author?" I asked, as he handed the book to me. "Guy Johnson. I haven't heard of him either." I handed the six-hundred-page book back.

"You've heard of Maya Angelou right? Well, this is her son."

"I didn't even know she had a son who wrote books," I replied. "Is it a good book?"

"Yeah, it's about a black man who doesn't take mess from anybody, black or white, back in the day."

I laughed. "That does sound quite interesting. Maybe you can bring it so I can read it when you come back for Spring Break."

"I'll leave this one for you. I'll bring you the sequel, *Echoes of a Distant Summer* also. I got both of them for Christmas, but I'll be finished with this one before we head back home in a few days."

I was impressed that Everett was a speed-reader like me. "Have you decided where you are going to college?"

"No," he answered. "I am undecided about what I want to do with my life. I want to go to seminary school, and I also want to teach on the college level. But, I've also had the desire to get a degree in accounting, so, I really don't know yet. I have had some schools sending me information, and I've applied for some scholarships, based on my GPA, so, I guess I'll be going wherever I get a scholarship to."

"I hear you. I have been undecided about what I want to do as well. I applied for some scholarships, and hopefully I'll get one or two. Money for school is going to be tight since Auntie's medical bills have been adding up. So, I'll just have to pray God gives me what I need."

"I'm sure He will Serenity. You're smart. When we had classes together before I moved, you were the smartest girl in my classes. I used to love doing projects with you because we thought so much alike. We always made an A."

"I know. I hated it when you moved because everyone else I ended up partnering with didn't seem to care about getting a good grade, they just cared about getting it done."

"I've run into that a lot with my partners at my new school. You think Nana has any Oreos hidden in the cabinet?" he asked, getting up from the floor.

"I don't know, she probably does."

"I'm going to check. You want some?" he asked, standing in the hallway.

"If it's Double Stuff, bring me at least five. But don't let those bratty cousins of ours see you sneaking them. They like to eat up everything," I said. I'm sure my facial expression was showing exactly how I felt about those bad kids that my Aunt Shay didn't know how to control. They ran through Nana's house, tearing up stuff and getting on everybody's nerves but Shay's. She had to know they were bad, annoying and obnoxious because Nana loved kids, but she threatened to knock some sense into Shay's kids every time the family got together.

I went back to my book. I guess I was so engrossed I didn't notice I was being watched.

"So, this is where you hid yourself," my mother said.

I looked up, startled by the sound of her voice. "Yes, I needed a quiet place to read." I looked back down at my book, hoping she would just leave the room. She came and sat down on Nana's bed instead. And, I know she knew better, because Nana didn't allow anyone to sit on her bed.

"What you reading?" she asked, as she touched my hair that was in a ponytail.

"The Color Purple," I answered, trying not to sound annoyed. I hated when she touched my hair too, so I tried to hold my head down, so she couldn't see my facial expression.

"That's by Alice Walker isn't it?"

"Yes," I replied.

"You not going to give your mama a hug? I haven't seen you since Thanksgiving."

"Maybe later. I'm trying to finish this book. I have another one I need to read before school starts," I said as I turned the page to my book, and uncrossed my legs. A few seconds later, I crossed them again, because I was uncomfortable being in the room with her.

"You ashamed of me Serenity?" she asked.

I had to think about the proper way to answer the question. "Sometimes." That was all I could manage.

"Why? I made you, and you're perfect. You're smart, and pretty, and if it wasn't for me, you wouldn't be here," she said, while slurring her words, so I knew she had been drinking. I turned to look at her face. Her eyes looked funny, so I knew she was high as well.

"You're right Mama," I said, and looked at my book.

"So, why you ashamed of me Serenity?" she asked again, sliding down on the floor beside me, and putting her arm around my shoulder.

I was quiet for a few minutes, and there was an unnatural silence in the room.

"Hey Serenity, I found them!" Everett exclaimed as he entered Nana's room with a whole unopened bag of Double Stuff Oreos. "Oh, I can come back." He turned to leave the room.

"NO!" my mother shouted at him, as she got up from the floor and walked over to him. "You stay. I need to talk to the both of you." She put her arm around him, and walked him over to the chair in Nana's room. "Sit down!" she commanded Everett. Not knowing what to do, he looked at me, shrugged his shoulders and sat down in the chair.

My mother stood close to him as she began to ramble about how the family looked down on her because she drank and got high. She talked about how she used to be a track star in high school, and how colleges were looking at her. She talked about how she used to love to read, and how she made straight A's in school. She went on and on about her boyfriend who was a star athlete, and how she messed up, and got pregnant.

Everett and I looked at each other, neither knowing what to do, but wishing we could escape from the room.

"And then, the doctor told me I wasn't having one baby…he said I was having twins…and imagine how surprised the family was when you two arrived." She looked at Everett, and then at me.

"Twins…I am the only one in this generation to have a set of twins. Mama's brother had a set, but…"

My head started to swim. I believe Everett must have had the same feeling I did, because simultaneously, we both said, "TWINS!"

She looked at us and nodded her head. "Yes, the two of you are twins. But I couldn't take care of you. I was a junior in high school, so the family decided to split you up. It wasn't my idea, but, hey, you two turned out fine." She had a dumb look on her face I was getting ready to slap off, but Nana beat me to it. I hadn't heard her come into the room, but I definitely saw her yank my mother around by her arm and slap some sense into her, or at least I hoped she did.

"Stephanie Marie! What have you done?" Nana yelled.

Everett and I were still looking and not quite understanding what had just happened.

"What Mama? All I did was tell them the truth. They're old enough to know the truth now. We're all *family*. No need to keep secrets anymore…" Before she could finish her sentence, Nana had slapped her again.

"Shut your mouth, Stephanie! Don't you say another word!" Nana was dragging her towards the door. "You've got to go, and you've got to go now!" Nana was so angry I could see the red in her eyes.

"Wait Nana," Everett called after her.

Nana stopped for a minute, still holding on to my mother's arm.

"Is what she saying the truth? Are we twins?" he asked pointing at me, then back to himself.

Nana put her head down, and looked at the floor. For a second, she released the grip she had on my mother's arm. "Yes, Everett, it's true. Serenity is your twin sister. We…the family was going to tell you when the time was right, but year after year passed, and it was easier to let you keep thinking you were cousins. The only reason why Serenity knew Stephanie was her mother is because she told her one day when she was high. You were hardly around her, so you got spared this drama you witnessed today. Now, I'm sorry you had to find out this way. I truly am."

I could feel the tears forming in my eyes. I ran out of the room to find my auntie. Everett followed me.

"Auntie Sheryl, why didn't you tell me the truth?" I shouted, when I found her at the kitchen sink, washing dishes.

"Tell you the truth about what Serenity? Calm down," she said.

Everett spoke before I could, "The truth about Stephanie being our mother. The truth about us not being cousins…the truth about us being twins," he said, as he turned to look at Aunt Sarah, the woman he'd called mama since he was six months old.

The only good part about that Christmas, was finding out my cousin, was my twin brother, which would explain why we looked like twins.

MARTIN

Simone and I had a nice evening planned for New Year's Eve. She and I hadn't spent much time together over the previous weeks because our work schedules were so hectic.

As I placed my last letter in the envelope and sealed it, I shut my computer down, ready to call it quits for the day. My phone rang, but I ignored it. If it were something important, whoever it was would call my cell.

I wanted to leave in time to stop by the post office to mail the letters. It was another bad weather day, but I had already made it to work when the snow began to fall.

As I carefully drove down the street, trying to avoid an accident I thought about how my brother and I loved to make snowmen when we were growing up. We used to have contests to see who could make the biggest. He usually won.

After I mailed the letters, I stopped by mama's house to see if she needed anything. I hadn't heard from her all day, so I wanted to make sure she was okay.

I knocked on the door, and after a few minutes, let myself in with my key. The house was quiet.

"Mama, are you here?"

She didn't answer.

I walked down the hallway to her bedroom, and she was lying in bed asleep. I walked over and sat down beside her. I gently touched her and called her name.

She woke up, and looked at me.

"Hey Martin. What are you doing here?" she asked, reaching for my hand.

"I came to check on you. I hadn't heard from you all day, so I came by to make sure you were alright." As her hand touched mine, I could feel she was hot.

I touched her forehead. "Mama, you're burning up with fever!"

"I'm just a little under the weather, that's all." She tried to sit up, but I urged her to lie back down.

"Did you take some medicine?"

"Yes, I took some earlier. But it's probably time for some more. I may have a touch of the flu. I didn't get my flu shot this year, and this is how I felt the last time I had the flu."

I got up from her bedside and went into the kitchen to see if she had orange juice and soup. She didn't have either. When we were growing up, and she thought we were sick, she'd give us chicken noodle soup, saltine crackers and orange juice.

I went back to her room. "Mama, I'll be right back. I'm going to the store to pick up some things for you."

"Thank you Martin. I didn't have the energy to go."

After I got mama situated with medicine and nourishment to battle the flu, I headed over to Simone's apartment.

She must have been running late because we pulled into the parking lot at the same time.

"Hey Sweetie," she said as she walked towards me. We hugged, as we walked towards the building.

"You have any hot chocolate?" I asked, as we entered her apartment.

"Check the pantry. I think there's some in there," Simone said as she took off her coat, and draped it across the sofa.

"I went by to check on mama. She thinks she's coming down with the flu." I found the hot chocolate and was making us a cup.

"She may need to go to the doctor. That flu is bad this year."

"I know. I went to the store and got some medicine, juice and soup for her. I'll check on her tomorrow. If I go by, and there's no greens, ham and black eyed peas cooking when I walk in the house, then I'll know she's really sick." I sat down at the counter, and Simone joined me.

"What time do we need to be at the party?" I asked, not really wanting to go, yet at the same time, not wanting to disappoint Simone.

She took a sip of her hot chocolate. "It starts at nine, but I know you really don't want to go."

"If the weather wasn't bad, I wouldn't mind, but you know I'm not trying to get into an accident."

"Well, we could just stay here, fix some dinner, watch a movie, and catch up on what's been going on with each other," she said, getting up from the chair. She went to the refrigerator to see what she could cook.

She was a very beautiful woman. I loved watching her, because she was so confident and classy.

"We could order some Chinese from the place down the street, so we don't have to wash dishes when we finish," I recommended. I was starving and didn't want to wait along time for meat to thaw out.

"Okay. You call, and place the order. I want Orange Chicken and Crab Rangoon, and I know you're getting Beef with Broccoli." She headed down the hallway. "I'm going to get out of these work clothes."

About twenty minutes later, the delivery guy knocked on the door.

We had a romantic meal in front of the window that overlooked the city lights. The snow was falling hard, and was blanketing the surface below. We talked about work, and her family. We talked about the cruise we wanted to take whenever we had the time.

"We're going to meet the girls in a few weeks," I said, as we cleared away our containers. "Mama is really anxious."

"I'll bet she is. I would be too if I were meeting my grandchildren for the first time."

"She wanted to meet them at the house, but I told her we should meet them at my office first, and set up a second meeting at the house at a later time."

"That's a good idea." We moved towards the living room and found a movie to watch.

We woke up the next morning, still on the sofa with the television on. We missed the New Year's ball drop, and we missed our new years kiss. Evidently we were both tired, and had fallen asleep before the movie was over.

The snow had begun to melt so I made my way to mama's house.

I walked into the house to the aroma of ham, black-eyed peas and greens. Mama was feeling better. She never let a New Year's Day go by without cooking this meal.

I walked into the kitchen and kissed her on the forehead. "Hey Mama. I see you're feeling better today." I reached for a piece of hot-water cornbread.

"Yes, I am. I guess that orange juice and soup, and that horrible tasting medicine you got me yesterday did the trick." She stirred the pot with the peas in it.

"Is it almost ready?" I asked, walking over to the television to see who was about to score on the football game.

"Yes, we should be ready to eat in fifteen minutes." She sat down on the sofa, and draped a blanket over her lap.

"I mailed the letters to the girls yesterday. So, hopefully they will call to set up an appointment time to meet with us soon."

"That's good. I've been wondering how Admire is doing. I'll be real glad to know she is alright."

"Me too, Mama. Me too."

MARTIN

January 20, the Saturday we were scheduled to meet with the girls seemed to come quickly. I'd sent a letter to the girls, giving them each a specific time to come to my office and meet with the scholarship committee for a face-to-face interview.

No one had called to say they couldn't make it. That was a good sign, especially for Admire, whom mama thought wouldn't come because she had been in the accident.

Mama and I had breakfast that morning at her house, before driving to my office. She was so nervous she changed her clothes three times.

"Mama, why do you keep changing?" I asked, getting annoyed because I hated to be late.

"Because, you only get one chance to make a good first impression, and I want to make a good impression on these young ladies…my granddaughters."

"Okay, Mama. But we are going to be late, and I hate being late." I stood by the door, with my hand on the knob.

"I'm coming. Start the car, I'm on my way out the door!" she yelled from her bedroom.

The first appointment was with Admire at 10am. Mama started to get impatient at 9:45am because Admire hadn't made it.

"Do you think she forgot? What if she didn't get the letter?" mama said, as she paced the floor to my office. She began to eat the M&M's in my candy dish, specifically only eating the brown ones.

"Mama, settle down. It's not ten yet, and you know that most people never make it anywhere on time. They are usually ten to fifteen minutes late," I said, as I checked my computer for emails.

Admire wasn't ten to fifteen minutes late. She was actually right on time. She rolled herself into the lobby of my office at ten o'clock sharp, and was escorted by her mother and stepfather.

I extended my hand to each of them, as I introduced mama and myself.

"I'm Martin Wilson, and this is my mother, Helen Wilson." Mama shook hands with Admire and her parents.

I invited them into my office and explained to the parents we wanted to speak with Admire alone, to ask her a few questions, and I explained we would schedule a final date to award the scholarship in the upcoming weeks.

"So, does that mean she definitely will get the scholarship?" her stepfather asked.

"I would like to say with certainty that she will get a scholarship, but there are some things we will need to do before we can give you a definite answer. Now, if you will please, make yourselves comfortable, we won't take up too much of your time. Admire, we're going to meet with you in my office," I said, walking ahead of her.

Mama couldn't take her eyes off of Admire. I'm not sure what happened to the plan I had created to follow a printed list of questions, get the young lady to allow us to take a swab of her mouth, for insurance purposes, and move on to our next appointment.

Somehow, mama took over. She asked Admire to tell her something about herself that wasn't in the essay. She asked her about the accident, and if she was making any progress with walking. Mama had her smiling, and acted as if she had known Admire longer than fifteen minutes.

I managed to get the chance to do the mouth swab, and get mama to realize it was almost time for our next appointment.

As we escorted Admire back into the lobby, I told her parents they would be hearing from us within a few weeks.

Mama couldn't resist the urge to hug Admire. "You are a beautiful young lady, and no doubt very intelligent. Keep believing in yourself, and I believe God will grant you the desires of your heart." She kissed Admire on the forehead then walked over to shake her parent's hands.

"Thank you very much for this opportunity, Mr. and Mrs. Wilson. I look forward to hearing from you," Admire said, as they opened the door of my building to leave.

Our next appointment was at twelve noon with Myracle. Mama was so anxious she kept going to the window every time she heard a car door slam.

At 12:05pm, Myracle walked into my office.

"Mr. Wilson," she said, extending her hand to shake mine. "I'm Myracle Lee. I'm sorry I'm late. I had a hard time getting my car to start. It's kind of old, a Volkswagen Bug. I got it for Christmas."

"That's totally understandable," I said, as I shook her hand. I had a flashback to the conversation my father had with my brother and I when we were younger. He said, "Son, when you meet somebody, look them square in the eye, state your name proudly and shake their hand like you mean it. People respect you when you show you are proud of who you are."

Myracle was a very beautiful young lady.

"This is my mother, Helen Wilson."

As Myracle extended her hand to mama, mama opted for a hug instead. She was face-to-face with the teenage version of herself. "Hello Myracle," she said, as she delicately hugged her. "It's nice to meet you. I've been looking forward to this for a while."

"It's nice to meet you too, Ma'am," she replied, not seeming to mind the hug at all.

"Well, let's meet in my office," I said, as I led the way down the hall. As we entered my office, I motioned for Myracle and my mother to have a seat. "Would you like something to drink," mama offered, unable to take her eyes off of Myracle.

"No, thank you. But, if you don't mind, I would like some of those M&M's," she said, not seeming shy at all.

I slid the bowl towards her, and said, "Please, make yourself at home." I was glad to see she was a lot more comfortable than Admire had been. I really liked her personality, as she sat there chatting with mama as if she had known her for longer than ten minutes. It was rather interesting watching her eat the M&Ms, as she only selected the brown ones. The only other person I had ever seen eat M&Ms that way was mama.

After I explained to her the need to swab her cheek for insurance purposes, I told her we would contact her again for the date and time of the dinner we would have to present her with the scholarship.

"So, I am definitely getting the scholarship?" she asked with a huge grin on her face.

"Yes. Myracle. You are definitely getting a scholarship," mama answered, smiling almost as hard as Myracle.

As she got up to leave, she turned and hugged mama and extended her hand to me again.

"Thank you so much!" she said. "This means a lot to me, and my grandparents. They are going to be so happy."

"Congratulations," I said, shaking her hand.

As mama stood in the window, watching Myracle drive down the street in the purple bug, she turned and said, "That young lady has a lot of character! I am going to enjoy being a grandmother."

I smiled at her, as I looked at the clock on the wall.

"Yes, I liked her too. She wasn't shy, or reserved. She was just naturally cordial," I commented.

"Her grandparents did a good job raising her," mama decided, as she nodded her head.

We were supposed to meet with Serenity at 1:30pm. It was 2pm, and she hadn't called, nor had she shown up.

"Maybe you should call her," mama said. "Maybe she forgot, or maybe she didn't get the letter."

"Okay, Mama." I dialed the number on her application, and waited for someone to answer.

"Hello." A voice on the other end said.

"May I speak with Serenity please?"

"Who's calling?" the lady on the other end asked.

"My name is Martin Wilson, and I had an appointment scheduled with her for today about the L.M. Wilson Achievers Scholarship she applied for. She hasn't shown up yet, so I was wondering if she needed to reschedule, or if maybe she forgot?"

"No, I didn't forget, and I don't need to reschedule," said the voice.

"Serenity, is that you?" I asked.

"Yes, Sir."

"Do you need a ride?"

"No, I don't need a ride. My family is having some issues right now... my auntie is in the hospital. Her cancer is back."

"I'm sorry to hear that Serenity. I can come pick you up if you need a ride?"

"No, I wouldn't want you to go through any trouble for me."

"It's no trouble at all. Is there an adult there with you? If so we could meet you at your home."

"My uncle is at the hospital with my aunt, but it's okay if you come here. He should be coming back within the hour."

"Alright then. My mother and I will be there in 20 minutes," I said, as I closed up her file, and placed it in my briefcase."

After I gathered everything I needed, mama and I headed to my car. Just as I got ready to lock the door to my building, my cell phone rang.

Trying to multitask, I dropped my phone on the ground. "Dang!" I exclaimed.

"Martin, what did you say?" mama asked from a few feet away.

"Dang, Mama. I said *dang*," I responded, grinning at her for acting as if I was still a little child.

"Don't you be grinning! And don't use that word. It's too close to the other one."

"Which one, Mama?" I asked, trying to make her slip up.

She looked at me and pointed her finger at me, as she waited for me to put my phone back together. "Martin, don't play with me."

"Yes Mama," I said, as I walked over to the car to open the door for her. As I got in the car, and turned it on, I tried to adjust the heater so the car could warm up. "It's too cold!" I exclaimed. "I'm ready for spring."

"I am too. This cold weather has my arthritis acting up a little. I still think I have a touch of that flu bug too."

I managed to put my phone back together, and as soon as I did, my phone rang again.

"Hello."

"Hey Martin," said a voice accompanied by sobs.

"Simone, what's the matter?"

"It's my sister. They had to rush her to the hospital this morning. They aren't expecting her to pull through this time. The doctor is saying she has maybe a few months at the most."

"I'm sorry to hear that. Where are you?"

"I'm on my way to the hospital. Where are you?"

"I'm on my way to meet with one of the young ladies at her house. If you want, I can come to the hospital when we finish?"

"No, I will call you later. Tell your mother I said hello."

"Okay. I'm sorry...truly sorry. I know what you are going through."

"Thank you. I know you do."

As we pulled in front of the house at 2211 Barber Street, I saw a face peering from behind the curtain in the front window.

Before we could get to the front door, Serenity opened it. "Hello," she said, watching us walk up the driveway. She was standing on the porch wearing warm-ups and socks.

Mama whispered to me, "She's going to catch pneumonia!"

"Hello," I replied. I extended my hand to Serenity. She softly shook mine, then turned to mama and shook hers.

"Serenity, I'm Martin. We spoke on the phone. This is my mother, Helen Wilson."

"You certainly are a gorgeous young lady," mama replied.

"Thank you Ma'am. Would you like to come inside?" she offered.

I nodded, "Yes, thank you for your hospitality."

We walked into the house, which was nicely furnished. There were lots of pictures of Serenity on the walls, and figurines of angels on the bookshelf. There were also a lot of healthy potted plants by the front window. Someone here definitely had a green thumb.

"You can have a seat, Sir," she said, making me feel old.

"Thank you," I said, as we took a seat on the sofa. She sat in a chair across from us, and nervously twisted her hands in her lap.

"We won't be long, as we understand your mind is probably somewhere else. I just wanted to do a quick swab of your cheek for insurance purposes... umm, regarding this scholarship, and ask you a few more questions."

"Okay. What else do you want to know?"

"Have you decided where you want to go to school yet?" mama asked.

"No, I guess it depends on my aunt's health. I would hate to be far away from her, I would worry too much. She's been dealing with this cancer stuff for years, and always manages to pull through. I will probably stay home, and go to the community college, in case she needs me."

"Your essay seemed so straight forward, Serenity. You seem to be a very mature young lady. How are things with you and your mother, if you don't mind me asking?" I asked. I was curious since she'd mentioned in her essay her mother had a drug problem.

Serenity's body language changed, as she readjusted herself in the chair. "Actually, I…my mother and I aren't exactly on speaking terms right now. That's…all I can say. I pray for her, but I don't have anything to say to her."

"Oh, child, that's a very grown up way to deal with things," mama said. "Did your aunt and uncle teach you that?"

"Yes, along with my Nana. I listen to the preacher at church sometimes. We attend the 2nd Baptist Church on 9th Street. But I was taught to pray for my biological mother from the time I learned who she was. Nana said we as a family had to pray for her, just in case she wasn't in the right mind to pray for herself."

I could see this was a touchy subject so I tried to lighten the mood.

"Well Serenity, I would like to inform you that you are going to receive a scholarship from the L.M.Wilson Achievers Foundation."

"For real?" Serenity asked, in disbelief.

"Yes. We will be calling you so you can attend a dinner where you will get the details of your scholarship."

Serenity stood up, with tears in her eyes, and said, "Thank you very much. This means a lot. I actually almost didn't apply for the scholarship. My counselor kept bugging me about it. And then I thought I had the worst essay…and I couldn't find a decent picture to send…but thank you. Thank you so much. I can't wait to tell my aunt and uncle."

"Who was the young man in the photo with you?" mama asked, as I prepared to swab Serenity's cheek.

"It's a long story," she sighed, and went on. "All my life, I was taught he was my cousin." She looked down at her feet. Then back up at us. "But Christmas day, I found out my whole family had been lying to us all of our lives. It turns out we are actually twins raised by different siblings. I was raised by my mother's older sister, and my brother, Everett, was raised by my mother's oldest sister."

"Oh my goodness!" mama said, unable to contain herself.

That was my cue it was time to go, because now I had to figure out a way to get in touch with Everett.

"Well, we must be going," I said, looking at my watch. "I will be in touch with you. Congratulations again. You are an amazing young lady, and I hope this scholarship will help make your life a little easier, in the future."

We shook hands, but mama walked over and put her arms around Serenity.

Serenity must have needed that hug, because she not only began to cry, but she tightly held onto mama for a few minutes. Mama patted her on the back, and told her everything was going to be just fine.

"I hope so, Ma'am. I hope so," Serenity responded, wiping the tears from her face, as their hug came to an end.

As we drove away, I could see out of the corner of my eye tears falling from mama's eyes.

"What's wrong, Mama?"

"That girl has had to be strong for a long time. She is mature. Very mature. I hope and pray we can help her, not just financially, but... spiritually...emotionally. I know she's been through so much in her young life. I want to help her, if I can, find some joy in her life. Her eyes are so, sad. Such a beautiful face, with such sad, brown eyes."

MYRACLE

I was so excited about winning the scholarship I didn't realize how fast I was driving. When I saw the blue and red lights flashing behind me, I almost had a heart attack.

I pulled over to the shoulder of the road and then made sure I had my seat belt on. I definitely didn't need a seat belt ticket, in addition to a speeding ticket. I could hear Grand D's mouth now, fussing about my foot being heavy and how, "the numbers on the speedometer are there for a reason; they match the numbers on the white boards with the black writing. Whatever number is on the speed limit sign, you need to be driving five less than that!" Man, I was going to get it.

The police officer walked up to my window. It was so cold outside that the tip of his nose reminded me of Rudolph the Red Nosed Reindeer.

"Good afternoon young lady," he said.

"Good afternoon, Mr. Officer."

"I need to see your driver's license."

I fumbled through my purse and finally found my license, which wasn't where I normally put it.

"How do you say your name, young lady?"

"Myracle."

"Well, Miss Myracle. I stopped you because you were speeding back there. You were going sixty-five in a forty speed limit zone. Are you late for an appointment? Or are you just a fast driver?" He handed my license back, as he smiled at me.

"Sir, I just found out I am being awarded a scholarship for college, and I was so excited, I guess I was driving too fast. I was trying to get home to tell me grandparents."

"Well, congratulations Miss Myracle. I don't want to spoil your good news for them, with the bad news of a ticket, so, I'm going to let you go, with a warning."

The biggest smile came across my face. "Oh, thank you Mr. Officer. I promise, I will slow down."

"Alright, young lady. Drive safely." And with that, he went back to his car, and I slowly drove home in mine.

When I got home, Uncle Terry was there too.

They were all sitting around the dining room table eating pecan pie Granny made for Sunday dinner.

"I hope you saved me some pie," I said, as I took my coat and scarf off, and hung them on the coat rack by the door.

"I saved you a piece," Granny said. "Your Uncle Terry was trying to eat it all up. Looks like I may have to make another one for tomorrow."

I walked over to the dining room table and sat down. All eyes were on me, as the family waited for me to tell them some news.

Grand D looked at me, with his head tilted to the left. "So, what happened?"

"I got the scholarship!" I screamed with excitement.

"That's great," Granny and Uncle Terry said at the same time.

"How much is it for?" Grand D asked.

"I don't know yet. They are going to call me to meet at some dinner and they will tell me then."

"Were you nervous?" Uncle Terry asked. He had just cut another piece of pie and placed it on his plate.

"No, not really. It was a lady and her son. The son is an attorney. They were really nice people."

"Well, congratulations Baby. I guess you deserve pecan pie and vanilla ice cream." Granny said, as she got up to go to the freezer.

"I looked in the freezer when I ate my first piece, Mama. I didn't see any vanilla. Sorry Miss Scholarship winner. I guess your pecan pie will be a little dry," he laughed as he took a big bite.

Granny moved some stuff around and when she came back to the table, she had a carton of vanilla ice cream in her hands.

"Mama, you hid that from me?" Uncle Terry asked.

Granny laughed and shook her head. "No Terry, I didn't hide it from you, I just put it where I knew you wouldn't be able to find it."

I called up my friends and told them I won the scholarship. They were excited for me. My mother called, and I heard Grand D in the other room excitedly telling her I won the scholarship.

Before I went to bed that night, I glanced over at the picture of my father. I wondered what he would have thought about me getting the scholarship.

Grand D came into my room, just as I was about to turn out the lamp for the night. He stood by the door, and said, "I'm proud of you Myracle. Real proud. I told your mama, and she said she was proud of you too. Keep your head focused on your future, and you will be just fine. Just like your mother. She was always focused. Knew what she wanted, and didn't let anything or anyone stop her. You are like her in a lot of ways."

"Thanks, Grand D. But, I don't know if I want to be like her. The part of her I know is…selfish and cold. Sometimes, I wonder if she really loves me, or if she blames me for…messing up her life by getting pregnant at a young age. She just doesn't seem to show me the love you and Granny and Uncle Terry do. It's just not the same. My friends and their mothers have a good relationship. I'm closer to my grandmother than I am to my own mother. You and Uncle Terry have been my daddy. My birth parents, the people who made me…I thank them for my good looks and my smart genes, but…I thank you, Granny and Uncle Terry for the rest. For all the stuff that makes me a good person, a good student, a person who loves herself, you, Granny and Uncle Terry helped mold and shape me."

"You are going to be alright little girl. It don't matter that your mama ain't the best at showing you love. That's why God gave you grandparents and an uncle to fill in the gaps, where your mama is lacking. Some mamas don't know how to show love. It's in their hearts. It has to be because they made you, and carried you close to their heart for nine months. And the heart is where love grows and lives. I know you think about it, but try not to let it worry you. Everything is the way it's supposed to be. The way God intended for it to be. And, I'm glad that I had the opportunity to help raise you." Grand D walked over to my bed, and kissed me on my forehead. "Good night, little girl. God's got great plans for you. Just you wait and see."

"Goodnight Grand D."

He walked out of my room, then turned around, and said, "And one more thing…"

"Yes sir?"

"Slow your butt down! Don't you get a ticket with your heavy foot."

"Who told you?" I asked, surprised he knew.

"That police officer who pulled you over is the one who used to own that little pink and purple car. I've known him since he was a boy. He went to school with your Uncle Terry. He called to congratulate us because you got a scholarship, and he told me that he pulled you over. He said he never planned to give you a ticket. Said you were so polite and nervous. He said even if he wanted to give you a ticket, he couldn't have because that charming personality and infectious smile wouldn't have let him."

I laughed. "I learned my lesson Grand D. I promise I'll slow down. That man almost gave me a heart attack when I saw his lights flashing in my rear view mirror. And, I could hear your speech in my head about the speedometer."

"You make sure you hear my voice in your head every time you drive. Put your seat belt on, no speedin', no talkin' on your cell phone while you are drivin', no fiddlin' with the radio while you're drivin', no puttin' on makeup while you're drivin'...just drive...that's it," he said, as he walked down the hall.

ADMIRE

My mother and stepfather wanted to go celebrate because of the good news that I was going to get the L.M. Wilson Achievers Scholarship. I was happy about the scholarship, but not happy about the possibility I would have to roll around a college campus in a wheel chair.

I wasn't a shallow person, but I didn't want people to feel sorry for me, or treat me like I was handicapped.

I wasn't handicapped. My legs weren't cooperating with the rest of my body at the moment. My legs weren't listening to my brain. My legs were acting like someone had put them in timeout for a long time. My legs... my legs were not being a team player. My legs were...not the legs that I ran with, jumped with, formed pyramids with and did cartwheels and somersaults with. My legs were like...the weakest link of my body. My mind was made up. My legs were not in charge of the rest of my body. My legs were going to have to do what my mind told them to do. My legs were going to take me wherever I wanted to go, and that was final!

"Let's go get ice cream. A Cookies and Cream sundae is in order for this special occasion," my mother said.

"I'm not really in the mood for ice cream, Mama. I have decided I am not going to college in this wheelchair. If I can't walk around a college campus, I'm not going. So, somebody needs to find me one of those hard core physical therapist people because I am tired of this wheel chair," I snapped.

My mother and stepfather looked at each other.

"Well," my stepfather said, "I guess we will save the ice cream party for another day. You want a tough physical therapist? You got it. No more Mr. Nice Guy! I am about to be your worst nightmare!" he said, glancing at me through the rear view mirror.

"What are you talking about?" I asked. "You aren't a physical therapist. I'm talking about some real, Billy Banks, Taebo king wannabe." I said, rolling my eyes. I could feel my attitude getting worse by the minute. I was ready to get home so I could go to my room and be alone.

"Your stepfather was a physical therapist in the Army. He just doesn't practice it much now, but he was very good at what he did." My mother didn't like it when I was in a bad mood. She said that was the worst part about me was the funky attitude I could get when things weren't going my way. And right now, not being able to walk was not agreeing with my spirit. I had pep talk after pep talk with myself, trying to convince myself this was God's plan for my life. But, I had also convinced myself this was only His plan for a little while, because He was waiting for me to use my determination and perseverance skills to change my circumstance, rather than letting my circumstance change me for good.

"Okay. Whatever. I've got nothing to lose," I said, rolling my eyes at the same time.

"If you cooperate and believe in yourself Admire, you will walk across that stage at graduation and give your valedictorian speech! I promise. If it is to be, it is up to me. That's what you need to say to yourself…If it is to be, it is up to me…if it's meant for you to walk, it is up to you to push yourself to make it happen."

I sat in the backseat as we pulled into the driveway at home, and I thought about the Serenity Prayer my grandmother used to make me recite when I spent the night with her.

"God, please help me change what I can, and bless me to know if it's supposed to be changed. If it's not supposed to be changed, then bless me with peace to be okay with it. Amen."

Physical therapy began the next morning at six! My stepfather woke me up and gave me a piece of paper that told me what I could expect.

I didn't expect to get up at six, but I was determined to make the best of this situation. If it didn't work, then it wouldn't be my fault for lack of effort.

That evening, my phone rang about nine o'clock. I was doing my homework and trying to finish before ten. I was tired and irritated at the same time.

"Hello," I said, as I answered the phone.

"Hey Admire. How are you?"

"Austin? What are you doing calling me?" I did not expect to hear his voice on the other end of the phone. I hadn't seen him at school or heard from him since my accident. It was like he vanished off the face of the earth.

"I...was wondering how you were doing?" he said, sounding nervous.

"Well, after a month of not hearing from you, you call wanting to know how I'm doing? I could be dead for all you know." I could hear my tone of voice getting louder.

"Yeah, I'm sorry I haven't called. But I just didn't know what to say. After I heard about the accident, I tried to come see you at the hospital but the nurse said only family could visit. Then, I heard at school that you couldn't walk, and I got sick to my stomach."

"Well, guess what? I've been sick to my stomach too. I thought you really liked me. I thought we were friends. But I guess I was wrong. There is no excuse for you not trying to call me for a whole month. I am busy right now. So, I have to go. Good luck with your life. And lose my phone number!" I yelled into the phone as I slammed it down.

SERENITY

I was happy to learn I was getting the scholarship I applied for, but I was still very upset with my family for keeping a secret from my brother and me.

I tried to reason in my mind how anyone could feel it was okay to split up twins, and raise them as if they were cousins for seventeen years.

My aunt and uncle tried to explain to me how neither family member was financially able to care for two newborn babies at the same time. They tried to make me understand how after years of raising us in separate homes, that it was just easier to let us believe we were cousins, than to try and explain we were twins. My uncle even took it a bit further and said if it wasn't for my biological mother opening up her big mouth when she was high one day, I would have never known I wasn't their biological daughter, because the family had originally decided to not share that information with us.

I knew Stephanie was my birth mother, but Everett had no idea. Somehow, she had never gotten around to letting the family secret slip when she was around him.

It felt so strange knowing I had a twin brother. We had always gotten along growing up. People at school often commented we looked like we could be brother and sister.

Nana and Papi always treated us special when we were growing up. Nana would keep Oreos hidden in the kitchen just for us. She made sure she had plenty of Cookies and Cream Ice Cream when she knew we were going to spend time at her house, and she gave us money for our birthdays.

On our birthdays, the family tried to play it off as a coincidence we had the same birthday. Of course, Everett and I thought it was cool growing up. It seemed to be a great occasion for the family, because there was always a big party for us and we had two birthday cakes, and got lots of presents.

I sat in the living room, alone after the gentleman and his mother left that day. I wanted to be excited, but I was too angry. I was also sad because my auntie was back in the hospital, and I was uneasy about the way Stephanie had blurted out the family secret. I had so many emotions going on in my head, all I wanted to do was lie down and go to sleep so I could stop thinking.

I hadn't been able to sleep much since Christmas. I don't know why, but when I lay down at night to try to sleep, my peace was interrupted by unhappy thoughts and conversations.

I was unhappy. I hated my biological mother, and at this point, I hated almost everyone in my family, accept my brother. I had thought about running away, but then auntie got sick, and honestly, I had no place to run to.

As I lay on the sofa, covered up with my favorite blue fuzzy blanket and watching Soul Train, the doorbell rang. I looked at the clock. It was almost four thirty.

I was surprised when I opened the door to find my brother Everett standing on the porch.

"Everett!" I said. "What are you doing here?"

"Mama got a phone call this morning from Uncle Thomas saying Auntie Sheryl was back in the hospital, so she drove down to see her. When I found out you weren't at the hospital, I asked her to drop me off here. I hate hospitals, and I really didn't feel like being around the family today," he said, as he took off his jacket, and plopped down on the sofa.

"I know what you mean," I replied, making myself comfortable in Uncle Thomas' recliner. "I'm still kind of mad about the whole thing. I haven't been able to sleep much. And, even though I feel bad Auntie Sheryl is in the hospital, I still believe the family should have told us the truth."

"Yeah, I agree Serenity. Mama tried to explain to me how it was best for the family that they keep it a secret. She said at first it didn't start out as a secret, but as we got older, and were treated like cousins, rather than siblings, it was easier to keep the secret a secret."

"But what if Stephanie hadn't told us? Would they have let us live the rest of our lives believing we were cousins? Do you recall how many times our friends have said we look so much alike we could be brother and sister?"

"Yeah, I remember."

"I know we can't change things now, but I wonder what it would have been like if we grew up knowing we were siblings."

"It doesn't matter. We both grew up in a nice home, with nicer parents than the one's who were responsible for us being here. We are both really good in school, smart, and we were blessed with good looks. So, all we have to do now is figure out how to move forward and get past this bump in the road." He got up, and headed for the kitchen. He was looking for snacks, and found the Doritos in the cabinet. He looked in the refrigerator and spotted the freshly made pitcher of Strawberry Kool-aid and set it on the counter, while he grabbed two cups out of the cabinet.

I followed. "I know you're right, but it's just not that easy for me. I love Auntie Sheryl and Uncle Thomas, but why couldn't we have been raised together? I don't know Everett. Maybe in time, I will feel better about this, but right now, I'm still angry." I grabbed a few chips from the bag, as we sat at the kitchen counter.

"The last time we talked, you told me you applied for some scholarship. Did you find out if you got it?" he asked.

"It's funny you should ask. Actually, I found out just this morning that I am getting the scholarship."

"That's good news," he replied, pouring another glass of Kool-aid. "So, have you given any more thought to where you want to go to college?"

"Not really. I guess things right now depend on Auntie Sheryl, and how things go with her health. I don't want to go far away, so I've been thinking about going to the community college. What about you?"

"I want to experience the college life. I don't want to go to community college. I feel like I've read about so many different places in books, I want to go out and make some history of my own. I applied to several colleges already; Morehouse, Tuskegee, George Washington University, Grambling and Harvard."

I looked at him with surprise on my face. "Harvard?"

"Yes, Harvard. I just want to see if I can get in. I applied to a lot of schools. I have also been applying for scholarships too. I don't want to have to pay back loans when I graduate. Mama said she knows this lady who is fifty-seven years old, and is still paying on her student loans from college."

"Well, I hope you get into Harvard, or wherever you really want to go."

"I'll get accepted to a few of them, the hard decision will come when I have to make the choice."

We spent the next few hours talking. It was getting late, and the Doritos were no longer curbing our appetite. So we ordered a pizza and played Monopoly.

Uncle Thomas called to see if we needed anything, and to say Aunt Sheryl was doing about the same. He asked if I wanted to go to the hospital. I told him no.

The next morning, when Everett woke up on the sofa, Uncle Thomas was in the kitchen making coffee. I was awakened by the aroma, and came out of my room to see who was making coffee.

"Good morning Serenity," Uncle Thomas said when he saw me. He looked tired, and was still wearing the same clothes he had on the day before.

"Good morning. How's Auntie Sheryl?" I asked, standing in the doorway of the kitchen.

"Well, little Princess," he said, "Your Auntie isn't doing so well. The… uh…doctor's are saying they've done all that they can do for her."

I didn't like what I was hearing. "So, what does that mean exactly?" I asked, as tears began to form in my eyes.

"It means, we need to love her and pray God spares her from unbearable pain as she prepares to leave this earthly home, for her heavenly home. That's what it means." He was getting choked up, and I saw tears forming in his eyes.

I didn't know what else to say. I just went back to my room.

I thought about praying, but I didn't know what to pray for. Undoubtedly, it was already decided that Auntie Sheryl was going to lose her battle with cancer. So, since asking God to heal her body was a waste of time, I asked God to take away her pain.

A few weeks later, God answered my prayer.

Auntie Sheryl passed away peacefully in her sleep, at home on Sunday, February 4.

The day before she passed away, she asked me to forgive her for not telling her the truth about Everett.

I told her I forgave her, and apologized for being angry with her.

I wasn't looking forward to the funeral. I had only been to one other funeral in my life, and that was Papi's. He passed away when I was eleven.

I missed school that week; just wasn't up to going. My friends from school came by to extend their condolences, and our family members from all over the state began to show up. The funeral was set for Thursday, and I was not looking forward to it.

People kept bringing food, mostly chicken. I was surprised to see Mrs. Wilson, the lady who came with her son that Saturday to tell me I was getting the scholarship, dropping off a pound cake.

I happened to be looking out the window when she drove up.

I opened the front door, and met her on the porch.

"Hello Mrs. Wilson."

"Hello, Serenity. I read about the passing of your Aunt in the newspaper, and I wanted to extend my condolences. I hope you like Sock-it-to-Me cake." She handed me the cake, which was loosely wrapped in foil. It was fresh too, because it was still warm.

"Yes Ma'am, it's one of my favorite cakes. Thank you for your kindness. Would you like to come in?" I asked.

"Oh, no dear. I can't stay. But, you and your family are in my prayers. If there's anything you need, please call us." She hugged me, and then walked back to her car.

As I watched her drive away, I realized strangers often helped ease my pain, when family had often been the reason for it. I made a mental note to send Mrs. Wilson a thank you card.

At the funeral, there was a lot of crying. I had cried a lot, thinking of how much I truly was glad she had raised me, instead of Stephanie, who for some reason didn't make it to her sister's funeral.

I saw Mr. Wilson sitting towards the back of the church, and he looked at me rather strangely.

At the cemetery, I noticed him talking to my Aunt Simone, and holding her hand.

MARTIN

Simone called early that Sunday morning to say her older sister, Sheryl had passed away.

Mama called me a few days later to tell me she saw in the newspaper that Serenity's aunt had passed away. Mama read the obituaries everyday.

I told her Simone's sister had passed away, and then we chatted about the weather and the Super Bowl game.

That Thursday, I was running late. I had an appointment with a client, and I wasn't able to get to the church in time to walk in with Simone. I hoped she wouldn't be angry with me.

I found a seat in the back of the church, which was full by the time I arrived.

I have to admit, I wished I could have missed the funeral, but I knew Simone needed me for moral support. She had taken her sister's death pretty hard.

We had talked for a few hours a few nights before the funeral about her sister, and how they used to be really close. Then she explained she had another sister, who was on drugs, and that the family had decided to keep some secret she didn't agree with. So, she had distanced herself from the family as much as possible. She didn't share the family secret with me though.

As I looked around the church, I noticed a familiar face staring at me. She looked puzzled, and as I realized who she was, I was puzzled as to why Serenity, one of the young ladies I had found out was my brother's daughter, was sitting with the family at the funeral.

At the cemetery, I saw the young man who was in the picture she sent in with her essay. Then, I saw the two of them, standing side by side.

Simone walked over to me, as I was staring at Serenity and the young man.

"Hey," she said, as she hugged me.

I hugged her back, and kissed her on the forehead.

"How are you?" I asked. "How's your mom?"

It was kind of chilly at the cemetery. And Simone was shivering, so I took off my jacket and draped it around her shoulders.

"Thank you," she replied, as she reached for my hand. We were walking down the path at the cemetery, away from the other family members. "My mom is doing…okay. She just keeps saying children are supposed to bury the parent, not the other way around. But, she said it must have been God's plan, so she can't argue with Him."

I looked at her tear stained face.

"And, you?"

She was trying to fight back tears, so she shook her head, and quietly said, "I'll be okay. It's her husband Thomas, who is taking it the hardest. They have known each other since elementary school."

"That has to be hard. I don't envy him at all, losing someone you love, and have loved for that long. How long were they married?"

"Twenty years. They got married right out of high school. She went on to the police academy after they got married, and Thomas went to college. They made a good life for themselves, and their daughter."

"Daughter?"

"Yes. See the pretty young girl over there in the black dress, with the green shoulder bag?" she said, pointing in Serenity's direction.

"The one standing next to the young man with the braids?"

"Yes. That's Serenity, her daughter. Well, long story…but anyway, Serenity is actually my sister Stephanie's daughter, but Sheryl and Thomas adopted her when she was born."

"And is the young man her brother?" I asked, after recalling my conversation with Serenity.

Simone paused for a few minutes, then looked at me, then back at Serenity and Everett.

"Actually, they are the family secret I was telling you about. They are twins, but my family decided to raise them believing they were cousins instead. I was against the idea, but no one in the family listened to me. So,

I distanced myself. I thought it was wrong. I understand they found out this past Christmas they are twins."

I could see this was a touchy subject for her.

"How are they, Serenity and her twin dealing with this news?" I asked, still holding her hand, and trying to decide if this was the right time to tell Simone my brother was Serenity and Everett's father.

"From what I understand, Everett took the news a lot better than Serenity did."

Later that night, after I had gotten home, and turned on the television, it hit me where I had seen the photo before that Serenity had sent in with her scholarship essay.

It was in the photo album underneath Simone's coffee table. I had flipped through it a couple of times while waiting for her to get ready for a date.

As I ate my ice cream, and a piece of the cake I had brought back from the repass, I wondered when would be the right time to share my family's secret with Simone.

If I didn't know any better, I would have bet anybody I was eating my mama's Sock-it-to-Me cake that night. Nobody made cake like my mama.

It was about a week after the funeral, and I was at work. My phone rang, and it was mama.

"Hello Mama."

"Did you get the results back on the DNA tests yet?" she asked.

"Oh, yes Ma'am. I got them back last week. It was just a formality, but they are all definitely Laramie's daughter's."

"Okay. Well, let's move forward with the plans for the dinner party. I'd like to do it Saturday, March 3. That will be the day after their 18th birthday."

"Mama, what if they have plans for the day after their birthday?"

"Well, they'll just have to change them. I am tired of waiting, and I want to get to know my grandchildren. By the way, what are you going to do about Everett?"

"Mama, there's something I need to tell you."

"Please don't tell me you've found out about another child we didn't know of." She sounded frustrated.

I tried to laugh, but it wasn't a laughing matter. And just as I was about to tell her what I needed to tell her, I noticed Simone walking towards my office.

"Mama, I am going to stop by this evening so we can talk more about this. I have to go now. Simone just walked in."

"Okay Martin. I'll fix dinner for you."

"That'll be fine Mama." I said, trying to get off of the phone. Simone had a look on her face I didn't like.

"Do you want chicken or pork chops?" mama asked.

"Chicken with mashed potatoes and green beans. Okay Mama. I love you. See you later."

Simone hardly ever showed up at my office without calling. I was wondering if she had found out about my family secret.

"Simone, what's wrong?" I asked, as I closed the door to my office. I sat down in the chair next to her, rather than behind my desk.

She looked at me for a few minutes, then looked towards the window and said, "My sister Stephanie is missing."

"Stephanie is missing? What do you mean, missing?" I asked, glad to know she hadn't found out my secret before I had the chance to tell her myself.

Simone grabbed a tissue from her purse. She had been fighting a cold all week. As she wiped her nose, she pulled out a folded piece of paper from her purse.

"She's missing. She didn't come to Sheryl's funeral last week. She didn't come to Mama's house after the funeral. No one has seen or heard from her since Christmas, when she caused a big scene after the Christmas dinner. No one knows where she is. So, my mother has filed a missing persons report, and she had my sister Shay make flyers to post around the city."

"Is there anything I can do to help?"

"Well, yes. I was wondering if you could call your friend, the private detective, and see if maybe he could help us. Mama isn't doing well. We just buried Sheryl last weekend, and now we don't know where Stephanie is. This is too much for her." Simone started crying. I tried to console her, but it only seemed to make matters worse.

"I'll call Harry this afternoon. Do you have any information I can give him, to help start his investigation?"

Simone handed me the folded piece of paper she had taken from her purse. "This flyer has the most recent picture of her that mama had, and on the back is some names and numbers and places mama had for people who normally know where she is."

"Okay. I will get this to Harry so he can begin to look into this." I placed the paper on my desk, and then decided this was as good a time as any to tell Simone my secret.

I turned to her, and took her hand, and looked into her eyes and said, "Simone, remember I told you I had found my brother's children? That I had gotten back confirmation through the DNA tests, and mama and I have met the young ladies?"

"Yes, Martin. I remember." She wiped her nose again, and looked at me, like I had her undivided attention.

"Well, one of those young ladies is your niece, Serenity."

She looked at me, kind of puzzled. "What do you mean?"

I walked around my desk, and opened my brief case. I pulled out the file folder containing Serenity's information and picture in it, and handed it to Simone.

"What's this?" she asked, looking at me, then at the folder.

"Open it." I sat down next to her.

She opened the folder, and saw Serenity and Everett's picture. She looked at me. "What is this?"

"Read it." I said, pointing to the essay.

"Oh my goodness! My niece and nephew are your brother's children?" She looked at me, then back at the picture of Serenity and Everett.

"Yes, Simone. I didn't know they were your niece and nephew until the funeral. I actually sat in your sister's living room with Serenity the day you called to tell me your sister was back in the hospital. When I went to the house to let her know she was getting the scholarship, she told me her aunt was in the hospital. I never made the connection. When I saw this picture, I kept thinking I had seen it somewhere. And it wasn't until that night, after the funeral, that I remembered seeing this picture in the photo album under your coffee table."

"This is so unbelievable! How small is this world, that my boyfriend is the uncle of my niece and nephew?" she laughed, a nervous laugh, then said, "Well, welcome to the family. Does she know? Did you tell her?"

"No. We are planning to have a dinner on March 3, and mama wants to tell them then. I would like for you to be there, too."

"I will have to think about it. I have a lot of things going on in my head right now, so, I'll think about it. I believe my niece has been through quite a lot these past few months. The mother who raised her, died last week. Her birth mother is missing. She found out her cousin is actually her twin, and now, she is going to find out that the father she never knew has died, but left her money to pay for college. I don't know if I could handle all of this, and I'm a grown woman."

I went to mama's house for dinner that night, and explained to her the connection between Simone and Serenity.

As I was getting ready to leave, she remembered to tell me she had received a thank you card from Serenity for the Sock-it-to-Me Cake and for stopping by to offer condolences after the passing of her aunt.

I knew that was my mama's cake.

MYRACLE

A letter came for me a few weeks before my eighteenth birthday. It was from the nice people who were awarding me the scholarship.

They were inviting me to attend a dinner the day after my birthday. At the dinner I would find out more details about the scholarship, and meet several other recipients of the scholarship.

I was asked to RSVP by the end of the week.

I called the phone number on the letter and left a message stating I would attend the dinner.

I had been trying to decide which college I wanted to attend. I applied to several really good schools, but was still undecided where I wanted to go.

My Uncle Terry wanted me to attend a historically black college, but Grand D said I should go to a college that looked good on paper.

My top choice was Spelman College in Atlanta Georgia, but I felt it was too far away from my family in Texas. Granny said it didn't matter how far away my pursuit of an education took me, I would never be too far away for my family to get to me when I needed them.

For my birthday, Granny fixed my favorite dinner, smothered pork chops, smashed potatoes and corn on the cob. I invited my friends, Sherice and Gammy, over that Friday night, and we decided to go to the movies after dinner. The new movie by Tyler Perry, *Daddy's Little Girls* was playing

We liked Tyler Perry, especially when he played Madea. Although he wasn't in this movie, we still wanted to see it.

Uncle Terry and his new girlfriend came over with a Cookies and Cream ice cream cake covered with Oreo cookies. It had to be the best thing ever made.

My mother didn't come by that night because she was working, but she called to wish me a happy birthday and said she would take me to breakfast the next morning.

Uncle Terry's new girlfriend was a beautician and offered to do my hair and my friend's hair for prom, which wasn't far away. We had already been looking at dresses online, because we wanted to get dresses no one else had. We wanted to stand out and be different and unique. We wanted to look back at pictures and see that we were the best dressed girls at the prom.

That night at the movies, we ran into some people we knew from school. There was a really cute guy there with braids. He was with his cousin. He kept looking at me while we were standing in the lobby waiting for the movie to start.

He looked familiar to me. Then Sherice reminded me he attended school with us a few years back. His name was Everett. I remembered him because he was really smart in the classes we had together. I wondered if it would be to forward of me to give him my phone number because I thought he might be a good candidate for my prom date. Sherice made the statement we kind of looked like we could have been related. I laughed at her, because she always thought somebody looked like somebody else.

After the movie was over, I saw Everett standing outside with Serenity, the girl from school. I was too shy to go talk to him, but Gammy walked over to him, pointed at me and gave him a tiny piece of paper.

When she came back, she said she had given him my number. I was so embarrassed.

The next morning, March 3, my mother picked me up at nine, and went to Waffle House for breakfast.

We made small talk, as usual, but I tried to remember what Grand D had told me. I tried to act like it didn't bother me that my mother and I didn't have a normal relationship.

I told her about the dinner I was going to that night, and she asked me what I was wearing. I hadn't thought about it much, but she said I needed to wear something new, so after breakfast, we went shopping for the perfect outfit.

She had to be at work by one o'clock, so she dropped me back at home around eleven thirty.

At five o'clock, I started getting ready for the dinner. I was supposed to be there at six thirty.

I was nervous, but tried to tell myself to just relax as I pulled up at the pretty, big white house. There were several other cars parked in front. I looked at the clock. It was 6:29pm, so I wasn't late.

As I walked up to the door, Mr. Wilson opened it before I had a chance to knock. He invited me to come inside, and as I followed him into the living room, I was surprised to see Serenity and that really cute cousin of hers, Everett.

ADMIRE

My stepfather was really patient while trying to help me walk again. It had been almost a month since we started the physical therapy, but I hadn't made much progress.

I had hoped to have the best gift of all for my eighteenth birthday, the ability to walk, but it didn't seem like that was going to happen.

About two weeks before my birthday, I received an invitation to attend a dinner given by the people who were giving me the scholarship. I thought about not going, especially since it was the day after my birthday, and I had already made plans with my friends to go to a play that was in town. Then, the week before my birthday, Lisa got grounded for sneaking in the house after curfew, so I decided to call and let Mr. Wilson know I would be attending the dinner.

For my eighteenth birthday, we went out to eat at my favorite restaurant, and the waitresses sang happy birthday to me, and brought me a Cookies and Cream ice cream cupcake with a candle on top.

When we got home, my stepbrothers brought a cookie cake into my room that had "Happy 18th Birthday Big Sister" written on it. I didn't even wait for my mother to bring a knife. I sat on my bed with my brothers, turned on The Cartoon Channel, and shared the cookie cake with them. As usual, they ate more of it than I did.

The next morning, as I lay in bed, wondering what I was going to wear to the dinner that night, my mother came into my room with a shopping bag from my favorite store. I sat up, as she handed it to me.

"What's this?" I asked, as she placed the bag on my lap.

"Open it," she said. "I thought you might like something new to wear to the dinner tonight."

She was right, and I loved the outfit that was in the bag. "Thanks Mom."

"You're welcome. I'm making pancakes for breakfast. You want to help?" she said, as she walked towards the door of my room.

"Sure. Let me get dressed first, and I will come help you."

At the breakfast table that morning, my stepfather was talking about a new exercise we were going to try that might help me gain some progress.

My stepbrother Jonathan looked at me and said, "Admire, are you mad at God because you can't walk?"

Andrew kicked him underneath the table, and said, "You aren't supposed to ask her that, Stupid!"

"You two, that's enough!" my stepfather said, with a look of embarrassment.

"It's okay," I said, looking at my stepfather, and then at Jonathan. "Every morning that I wake up, and can't walk, I get angry, but not at God. I heard somebody say once that what doesn't kill us, makes us stronger. I am glad I didn't die in the car accident, so I know I must be gaining strength in some form. Whether it's in my faith, or my prayer life, something positive is going to come from this. I don't know what, or when, but I have to believe something good is going to happen to me, to take the place of this... unfortunate circumstance I'm going through right now." A tear rolled down my face as I looked at the uneaten pancake on my plate.

My mother reached over and patted me on my hand, as Jonathan said, "I didn't mean to make you cry, Sis. I'm sorry."

I looked at him, through tears that seemed to keep forming in my eyes and said, "You didn't make me cry. So, you have no reason to be sorry."

I hated feeling sorry for myself, and I hated it even more when other people felt sorry for me. I wondered if the people were giving me the scholarship because they felt sorry for me.

As I got dressed, I wondered if God was listening to my prayers. I wondered if I wasn't being specific enough with my requests.

I wondered if, regardless of how much I believed in the power of prayer, I would ever walk again.

My mother pulled up to the house at 6:30 on the dot. I thought we were going to be late, because we couldn't find the address.

Mom got out of the truck and helped me get into my wheelchair.

"You want me to walk you to the door?" my mother asked me.

"No, I can do it by myself," I said. She kissed me on the forehead and stood by the car as I wheeled myself towards the front door. They must have been watching through the window, because Mrs. Wilson opened the front door before I had the chance to knock.

"Hello Admire," she said, smiling at me.

"Hi Mrs. Wilson," I said, smiling back at her.

She stepped to the side so I could enter the house. As I rolled into the living room, I saw two girls from my school. One was Myracle, the girl who saved my life by pulling me from the car before it caught on fire, and the other was Serenity, the editor of the school newspaper.

SERENITY

About a week after the funeral, Nana called the family together to tell everyone she had filed a missing person's report on my mother. She said it was unusual for her not to come around when Sheryl passed away, and none of the people who normally saw her, had recalled seeing her since Christmas.

Nana was nervous, and believed something bad had happened to my mother. She started blaming herself because she had slapped my mother Christmas night, after she told Everett and I we were twins.

I didn't want anything bad to happen to Stephanie, although I was still angry with her for the way she acted that night.

When we returned home after the family meeting, I went to the mailbox and found a letter from Mr. Wilson, the man who came to the house and talked to me about the scholarship I applied for.

I opened it as I walked into the kitchen, where Uncle Thomas was.

"What's that?" he asked, while pouring a glass of orange juice.

"An invitation to a dinner from the L.M. Wilson Scholarship Committee. It's the day after my birthday. They are supposed to let me know how much scholarship money they are going to give me."

"That sounds like good news, Baby Girl. And Lord knows we sure could use some good news around here."

"Yeah. I agree. These past few months have been crazy," I said, as I sat down at the counter. My uncle was always an easy person to talk to. "I have to admit I have been carrying a grudge with Stephanie and Auntie Sheryl since Christmas because of the secret the family has been keeping from me and Everett all these years. Didn't you think we should have been told we were twins?"

My uncle looked at me, then looked away. "Yes, Serenity. I thought you two should have been told you were twins. But Sarah didn't want Everett to know Stephanie was his real mother. They had attended a family gathering, and she found Stephanie in the room alone with him. He was five years old. She said Stephanie was holding him and saying crazy things to him, and Everett was crying and struggling to get away from her. She said after they got home, Everett told her Stephanie said some day she was going to tell him a secret. After that, Sarah never let Everett be alone with Stephanie. When she moved away a few years back, she said Stephanie had started blackmailing her and asking for money. Stephanie was threatening to tell Everett the secret that she was his mother. So, Sarah made sure Stephanie didn't have her phone number or her address."

"That's no excuse Uncle. We still had a right to know we were brother and sister." I looked at him and he shook his head.

"You're right Serenity. But, we can't change the past. Your aunts and your grandmother thought they were doing what was best for you and Everett. My argument was for the two of you. I felt you should know, but I lost the battle. The family has always tried to treat you and your brother special. Stephanie was fine with the adoptions until she started taking drugs. Some how, she got the notion she wanted the two of you back, but none of us would give in to her requests. Your grandmother tried to pacify her by giving her money whenever she asked for it so she would leave you and your brother alone."

"I hear you Uncle. I just…I just think we should've known. We can't change the past, but I wonder what did we miss out on by not knowing. I always wanted a brother, and oh my goodness, I had one all along. I always felt close to Everett, but I didn't understand why."

My uncle walked over and hugged me. "The wisdom to know the difference, Baby Girl. You have wisdom. You are very smart. You've always been. You are a beautiful young woman, with a bright future ahead of you. Don't allow this to eat you up inside. Let it go, and move forward with your life. Anger can make you bitter and old before your time. Find a way to move past this. You and Everett will have time now to make up for lost time. Hopefully, Stephanie will be okay, and we can focus on getting you ready for graduation and college. Your Aunt Sheryl made me promise her I would help you stay focused and help you reach your goals."

I hugged him back, and managed to smile at him before I went into my room to call my brother.

For my birthday, my family got together at Nana's house. Aunt Sarah and Everett were there. Aunt Simone stopped by earlier with presents but didn't stay. She said she had a meeting to go to.

Everett and I talked in Nana's room. Amazingly, no one interrupted us, and we spent our eighteenth birthday, as twins, rather than cousins. Nana had found our photo of the day we were born, and gave each of us a copy of it. I was wondering how this photo had managed to remain hidden from view for eighteen years.

"Do you want to go to this dinner with me tomorrow?" I asked him, as he ate another Oreo cookie. "I'm kind of nervous about going by myself."

"I'll go with you. I have nothing else to do, and I don't want to sit around here all day tomorrow with them while they talk about Stephanie. Have they found out anything? Has anyone seen her?"

"No, but I heard them talking. Aunt Simone has hired a private investigator to find her."

"Sounds intense. I hope nothing bad has happened to her. I always tried to avoid her, especially since she seemed to stare at me all the time. I guess now I know why she was staring at me. When she told you she was your real mother, how did you feel?"

"I was little, so I don't think I really understood what she was talking about. Auntie Sheryl and Uncle Thomas took care of me, and raised me, so whatever she said, didn't really make sense to me. I didn't like being alone with her. I guess the fact she was on drugs and always seemed to be high didn't sit well with me."

"Yeah, I was embarrassed at the fact she was my aunt, so I can imagine how you felt knowing she was your mother. Now that I know she is my mother too, I don't know what to think. I love my mom, Sarah, that's who took care of me, and encouraged me, and developed my sense of character."

The next day, Uncle Thomas let me use his truck to drive to the dinner at the Wilson's. Aunt Sarah was hesitant about Everett going, since he wasn't invited. But since the family secret had come out, and the family was feeling guilty about not being honest with us, Aunt Sarah gave in and said he could go.

As we pulled up at the house, Everett admired the nice black Mercedes in the driveway.

"That's Mr. Wilson's car. He's an attorney," I replied.

"There is fat money in that career choice," he responded, as we got out of the car. A car was pulling up behind us. As I strained my eyes, I recognized the face behind the wheel of the car. It was Aunt Simone.

She looked as surprised to see us, as we did to see her.

"Aunt Simone, what are you doing here?" I asked, as she walked towards us.

"Hi Sweetie." She kissed me on the cheek and then kissed Everett. "I'll explain everything later, but my friend's mother lives here."

"Yeah, I saw you and Mr. Wilson talking at the funeral. I was wondering how you knew each other."

"Long story, but let's go inside. I'm supposed to be helping with the dinner." She walked ahead of us, looking nervous.

She knocked on the door, and was greeted by Mr. Wilson.

"Serenity, how are you?" he asked, as he stepped to the side, and welcomed us into the house.

"I'm fine, sir. I hope you don't mind that I invited my brother Everett to come with me?"

Mr. Wilson extended his hand to Everett, and said, "No, I don't mind at all. In fact, I am glad you invited him. I'm sure he will benefit from this dinner as well. Please make yourselves comfortable," he said, as he and Aunt Simone walked down the hallway.

"Nice house," Everett said, looking at the bookshelf. "There must be over three hundred books here." He picked up one, and flipped through the pages.

"Yeah, I would love to read some of these," I replied, standing next to him, in awe of the number of books before me.

"Which one would you like to read?" asked Mrs. Wilson, who was standing behind us.

I turned to look at her. "Oh, it doesn't really matter. Any and all of them. I love to read, and so does my brother."

She walked over and hugged me, then looked at my brother for a few moments, and introduced herself.

"I'm Mrs. Wilson. And you are?"

"Everett Smith," he said, as he extended his hand to her.

She shook his hand, but hugged him also. "It's very nice to meet you, young man. Please make yourself at home."

We sat down in the living room, and glanced at the photo album on the coffee table.

I noticed Mrs. Wilson get up and walk towards the door. The doorbell hadn't rung, but she opened it, and Myracle, the girl we saw at the movies the night before, was standing there.

She came in, and sat down on the sofa next to my brother, as Mrs. Wilson made small talk.

A few minutes later, Mrs. Wilson went to the door again, and when she opened it, Admire, the girl who was in that horrible car accident was sitting there, in her wheelchair.

THE DINNER

Before dinner was served in the dining room, Mrs. Wilson sat in the living room making small talk with her grandchildren.

Simone and Martin walked into the living room, and Martin looked at his mother and told her dinner was ready to be served.

Mrs. Wilson got up from her chair and said, "Alright everyone, let's go into the dining room. I hope you are all hungry because we have prepared a special celebration dinner for you this evening." She led the way, as the others followed.

As they entered the dining room, they saw a feast of grilled pork chops, fried chicken, mashed potatoes, green beans, cornbread and peach cobbler on the table.

"Now, I know that all of you like Cookies and Cream ice cream, so we have some in the freezer, along with some Oreo cookies."

Everett and Serenity sat beside each other. Martin helped Admire get out of her wheelchair so she could sit in one of the dining room chairs between Mrs. Wilson and Myracle. Simone sat between Martin and Everett.

Martin decided that it would be best to let everyone finish eating first before telling the group of young people the truth about why they were all there. He and Simone had discussed it in the kitchen, and she was a little nervous about how they would react. She agreed there wasn't an easy way to break the news, but wished none of them had been put in this situation.

As dinner drew to a close, Mrs. Wilson went into the kitchen to get the ice cream and cookies. Simone helped her scoop out the ice cream into bowls and passed them to the grandchildren.

Admire looked at Myracle and said, "I never did thank you for saving my life that day. I had been meaning to, but I haven't seen you at school much these past few months."

Myracle took a bite of her cookie, and said, "It's no big deal I'm glad I was there to help. Are you going to be in the wheelchair much longer?"

"I hope not," Admire replied. "I'm doing physical therapy with my stepfather, so I hope to be walking by graduation."

"Well, let's hope for the best," Myracle replied.

"I was at the post office that day. And I saw you pull her from the car. That was a really brave thing you did because the car was already on fire," Serenity commented to Myracle.

Myracle looked down at her bowl, and shyly replied, "I would have wanted someone to do the same for me. So thanks."

Everett looked at Myracle and she blushed. "That's cool...really cool."

Simone began to notice sparks trying to fly between Everett and Myracle, so she looked at Martin and said, "I believe we should get to the reason they are all here. I'm going to start clearing the dishes from the table."

As she started clearing the dishes, all of the kids got up to help her. All except for Admire, who was trying to get into her wheelchair so she could go into the kitchen to help with the dishes.

Mrs. Wilson was surprised to see such polite and well-mannered young people in her midst. She didn't even try to stop them. Within twenty minutes, the table was cleared and the dishes had been washed and dried.

As they finished, Martin asked them to all come back into the living room so he could share some information with them.

After everyone found a seat, Martin took a deep breath, as he stood in front of the bookshelf next to Laramie's picture.

Myracle's facial expression changed as she recognized the man in the picture.

"Well, let's get on with it. First, I would like to thank each of you for coming here this evening. Ummm...I...well, okay, as you know, a few months ago, all of you, with the exception of Everett, applied for a scholarship. So, today we are here to explain the scholarship to you and answer any questions you may have." Martin looked at Simone, and then at his mother and sighed. This wasn't going to be easy he could tell. He had been a lawyer for ten years now, and had stood before people everyday making speeches, but this speech wasn't easy.

"This scholarship is named after my brother, Laramie Mitchell Wilson, who passed away this past November of cancer." Martin took another deep breath, pointed at Laramie's picture and continued. "Before my brother passed away, he asked me to find his children, whom he had never met because he was leaving them money to pay for their college education. And, well, here you all are. Everett, Serenity, Admire and Myracle. I am your uncle, and my mother is your grandmother. You are all the children of Laramie Mitchell Wilson."

The room was very quiet, and all of the children looked at each other in shock.

Mrs. Wilson got up from her chair and walked over next to Martin. "The meal you ate tonight was your father's favorite meal. Now, we didn't know anything about you until November. If we had known Laramie had children, we would have been a part of your lives. We can't change the past and the fact you didn't get to grow up knowing my son or us. However, we would like to try and make up for lost time. We want you to get to know us as your family. We want you, as brother and sisters to get to know each other. You all have so much in common. When we read your essays, much of what you wrote mirrored each other's essays. You are all beautiful young people, and I am glad to know I have grandchildren such as you. Your father was a high school football coach. On the coffee table are pictures of he and Martin when they were growing up. He loved to read, and a lot of these books are his. I would like for you to make yourselves comfortable around us. We just recently learned that Simone, who is Martin's girlfriend, is also Serenity and Everett's aunt, so I believe God intended for us to be apart of your lives, and for all of you to be apart of each other's lives. How ironic was it Myracle pulled Admire from a burning car, and Serenity was passing by as it happened? I know this is surprising information to all of you, but we didn't know how else to bring you together and share with you the blessing your father left for each of you."

"This is so weird," Myracle said, smiling nervously. "I have been asking my mother for years about my father. And this past Christmas, she gave me a picture of him. I have known of Admire, Serenity and Everett because we have all gone to the same school since we were in Elementary. But I would have never dreamt they were my brother and sisters."

"I agree. My friends have always said we all looked alike, and had asked me if I was sure we weren't related. And, here we are today, all finding out we are," Admire said, wiping tears from her eyes.

Serenity looked at Everett and said, "These past few months have been…so, strange. Everett and I have been raised all of our lives believing we were cousins, and just found out at Christmas we are actually twins. Now, I'm finding out I have two sisters as well. I'm not sure I can handle many more surprises. I would like to thank you again, Mrs. Wilson, for coming by and bringing that delicious cake when my auntie passed away," she said. Simone walked over and patted her on the shoulder.

"You're welcome," Mrs. Wilson replied.

"I think it's cool. I just came here today because my sister didn't want to come by herself. I guess it's a good thing I did, because I was planning on calling Myracle tonight to ask her on a date. So, since you're my sister, I guess I will be calling you anyway so we can hang out," he said, and everyone in the room laughed.

Mrs. Wilson smiled, as she looked around the room. She was glad that it seemed like everything was going to be okay.

Martin cleared his throat. "Now, that we have gotten that part of this meeting out of the way, and I'm sure you all still have questions, let me assure that each of you have a college fund I have set up with the money my brother left for you. There is more than enough money for the four of you to earn a four-year degree at whichever college you choose to attend. As you get closer to making your decisions, and begin to incur college expenses, just call me, and I will take care of them. Now, there are some stipulations. You are going to be expected to go to school, and finish school. When and if you finish college, whatever money is left from your college fund is yours. If you don't finish college, or choose not to go to college, I will give you a check for a certain amount, and that will be all you receive. Does anyone have questions?"

"I do," said Admire. "Why didn't our father help take care of us?"

Mrs. Wilson looked at Admire and shook her head. "I don't know what he was thinking, to be honest. I believe he got caught up with your mothers. He was a star athlete and was on his way to college. He said he didn't know they were pregnant until months later, and when he found out, he was ashamed and embarrassed to tell me."

"My brother made some foolish mistakes, but he admitted one of the biggest mistakes he made was not getting to know you, his children. He had actually decided a few months before he found out he had cancer that he wanted to make things right, and find you. He knew there were three babies, so I'm guessing no one ever told him there was a set of twins. After he found out he was going to die, he said he didn't want to come into your life for a brief period of time, only to have death take him away again. So, he asked us to fill in the gap in his absence."

"I was wondering if any of you were actually friends in school?" Simone asked.

Each of the children shook their head no.

"Well," Mrs. Wilson said, "everyone needs at least four good friends. So, who better to be friends with than your siblings? I truly hope this will be a positive moment in your lives, and I pray none of you will leave here today resentful or upset. I urge you to talk to us about what you are thinking, and feeling. We want to be here for you, if you let us."

Mrs. Wilson walked over to each of her grandchildren and hugged them. She then went back over to the bookshelf. She stood with her back turned to the others for a few minutes, but when she turned around, they could see she had taken the pictures they had sent in with their essays and blown them up to 8x10's, and had them framed. She had arranged all of their pictures on the bookshelf.

Myracle walked over to the bookshelf and looked at their pictures, and then at Laramie. "I guess we do look alike. My friends are not going to believe this."

"Mine either," Admire replied.

Simone had brought her camera and had been taking pictures throughout the evening. "Why don't we take one big group picture?" she said. "Let's get Mrs. Wilson in the middle, and Martin, you and Everett can stand in the back behind the ladies."

"So, what do we call you," Admire asked, as she looked at Mrs. Wilson.

"I don't know. This is my first time having to be called something other than Mama or Mrs. Wilson."

"I got it," Everett said. "Let's call her Mama Wilson."

"That sounds good," Myracle agreed.

"Yeah, I like it," Serenity replied.

"Okay, then," Simone said, "on the count of three, everybody say 'Mama Wilson'."

MAMA

I am so glad the dinner went well. After all the children went home, and I had a chance to sit in the living room alone, and look at the pictures on my bookshelf, I had the urge to find the letter Laramie had written to me before he died.

I read it again, and I cried, just as I had the first time Martin read it to me five months ago. However, this time, I believe some of my tears were tears of joy because although I had lost my son, I had gained four grandchildren.

I hoped they would call and want to come by. I was hoping they would remember me on Easter Sunday and Mother's Day. I wondered if they would invite me to graduation and other special occasions in their lives.

I had an instant connection with Myracle, and I believe once Admire got her spunky spirit back, she would be a lot happier. Serenity and Everett had a lot going on in their lives, especially since their birth mother was missing, and presumed dead. It had been three months since anyone had heard from her or seen her.

I prayed that night for my family, and before I went to sleep, I read the Serenity Prayer again, as it was displayed on a plaque on the dresser beside my bed. I read it over and over that night.

"God grant me the serenity to accept the things I cannot change, the courage to change the things I can, and the wisdom to know the difference."

I couldn't change the past, but I was ready to accept and change whatever I could in the present, to make the future better.

About a week later, Simone stopped by the house and brought a photo album she had put together from the dinner. She also had the group picture enlarged and framed.

"Here Mama Wilson, now you can hang this one up on the wall if you like," Simone said, smiling at me.

"It is so beautiful. And I truly appreciate your help that day," I said.

"It was my pleasure. I felt like I needed to be here for my niece and nephew. I talked with them after we left, and they seemed excited about college, and meeting everyone."

"Well, I'm glad. I was worried in the beginning, but hopeful. You never know how things will turn out when you're dealing with people's feelings," I said.

"I believe you and Martin handled this whole situation in a regal manner. Everything was done with taste, and very business professional, so as not to offend anyone. Very classy Mama Wilson. Very classy!"

"Thank you Simone. My main concern was for the children, and how this would impact them. I wanted things to turn out positive."

"I believe you got what you hoped for. Especially those grandchildren you always wanted," she said, smiling, as she kissed me on the cheek.

The following Saturday, I received an unexpected visit from Teresa. It had been months since we had talked, and I was glad to see her.

"I came down to visit my mother, and thought I'd stop by to see how you were doing," she said, as she hugged me.

"Well it's so good to see you. Have a seat," I said, as we made our way into the kitchen. I was in the middle of baking a cake, something I did most Saturday's.

"Looks like I'm just in time."

"Yes, you are. You can take this cake with you when it's done."

"I'll take a slice or two, but if I take the whole thing, I'll eat it all. And I'll have to work out twice as hard," she said. She was a very pretty woman. Shoulder length hair, slender, pretty eyes and perfect teeth.

"So, how have you been?" I asked her, as I slid the cake into the oven.

"Ok, I guess. I've been keeping busy."

"Well, I know how you feel. Let's go in the living room. I want to show you something. That cake will take a little over an hour to bake."

We walked into the living room, and I directed her attention to the bookshelf.

"This is what I wanted to show you," I said, pointing at the pictures of my grandchildren. "I know Laramie told you about his children, and these are their pictures. This is Myracle, Admire, Serenity and Everett," I said, pointing at each photo as I told her their names.

"So, Martin was able to locate them. But I thought there were only three?" She looked at each of the pictures, then at Laramie's picture.

"Yes, he was able to find them, and we originally thought there were only three children, but Serenity and Everett are twins. They are all very smart too. They are a lot like Laramie."

"The girls are beautiful. And, this boy looks so much like him. I know you must be so excited to have grandchildren around." We walked over to the sofa, and sat down.

"Yes, it is exciting. I was worried at first because I didn't think we would find them. Admire, the one in the middle, was in a car accident, and Myracle saved her life, but the accident left her paralyzed below the waist."

"Oh my goodness!" Teresa said, covering her mouth with her hand. "That's awful."

"We're hoping and praying she gets better."

Teresa saw the photo album on the coffee table and began to look through it. When she got towards the back, she saw the pictures that we had taken at my birthday party the month before Laramie died.

"This seems like a life time ago," she said.

I smiled at her. I looked at myself in the photo, and realized I had aged some since Laramie's passing. I had more grey hair, and a few bags under my eyes. I guess worry and sleepless nights do that to you.

"That cake sure does smell good," she said, as she closed the photo album.

I got up from my seat. "It should be ready," I said, as I headed towards the kitchen. I opened the oven, got the potholders from the counter, and placed my pound cake on the stove.

Teresa came in the kitchen and sat down at the table. "You want to play a game of Scrabble?"

I looked at her, surprised at her suggestion. When she and Laramie would come for a visit, we'd play Scrabble, and she was pretty good at it.

"That sounds like a good idea," I told her. "I'll cut the cake, you get the game from the closet. Do you want ice cream with yours?"

"Only if you have Cookies and Cream," she said, with a smile.

MARTIN

I was surprised at how well the dinner had gone. I was glad there was no drama, no one cussing at me, or screaming and yelling, the way they do on those talk shows. I was happy we had a nice, quiet family meeting.

Simone had been a big help, even though I knew she was really there because of the twins. I believe she was mostly concerned about Serenity because she had been going through so much with the passing of her adoptive mother, and now with her birth mother missing.

She came by my office a week later to bring me copies of the pictures from the dinner so that I could send them to the kids. That reminded me I had something else I needed to send to them. While she sat in my office, I looked through my brother's folder in my desk drawer and found three envelopes he'd asked me to deliver after I found his children. After realizing my brother never knew about the fourth child, I opened the envelope intended for Stephanie's child, and went to the copy room to make a copy of the letter for Everett. I went back into my office and found a picture of my brother to include in the letter that needed to be sent to Everett.

I placed copies of the photos Simone had brought and the envelopes containing the letters my brother wrote to his children inside four larger brown envelopes and addressed them accordingly.

"I need to go to the post office. Would you like to join me for lunch?" I asked Simone.

"Sure," she said. "Have you heard from the private investigator?" she asked as we walked down the street to the post office.

"No, but when I do, I'll let you know. How is your mother doing?"

"She's worried. She believes something bad has happened to her. She's blaming herself because of the fight they had that night."

"Well, hopefully we will hear something soon."

As we walked into the sandwich shop to get lunch, I realized how beautiful Simone was. I hadn't really paid attention to her the past few months with all of the things going on with my brother. I decided I was going to stop letting things get in the way of us. I decided I was going to ask her to marry me. And I did. Right then, and there, over a bowl of broccoli and cheese soup and a turkey, ham and cheese sandwich with lettuce, tomato, pickles and mayo on three cheese-baked Italian bread.

"Will you marry me?" I asked as she took a sip of bottled water.

She almost choked as she looked at me.

"What?" she responded.

"Will you marry me?" I asked again, this time, remembering I needed to be a little more romantic, and get down on one knee like they do in all the *Lifetime* movies.

As I got down on one knee, and grabbed her by the hand, I looked her in the eyes and said, "I love you, and even though I don't have a ring in my pocket to give you, I promise when we finish eating lunch we can go down the street to Zales, and you can pick out any ring you like."

She looked at me, smiled and said, "Any ring?"

I nodded, wondering what I had gotten myself into.

"Ok, yes, I will marry you," she said, as she kissed me on the lips.

It seemed corny, but people in the sandwich shop started clapping for us. And I suddenly remembered I had on an expensive suit and was getting one of the pants leg knees dirty.

"Okay, now, I don't want to wait a long time to do this either. Because if we wait, it will be just like all the times we talked about it before, but never got married," I told her.

"How about we get married in May," she responded.

"What? May? That's about a month away," I replied, taking a bite of my sandwich. "But ok. I guess it won't be a big wedding. Just small and simple."

She looked at me and smiled, "That's fine with me. My ring will be big and classy, so that's a fair trade."

About a month after the dinner with the kids, Harry, the private investigator called me to say the police had found some remains behind the bus station not far from Simone's mother's house. They were trying to identify them, and would let me know if it was Stephanie.

As I sat in my office, reading over a file I had already read twice, I wondered if the remains were Stephanie's, and if so, how did she end up behind the bus station not far from her mother's home.

While trying to focus on the file in front of me, I was interrupted by the phone. It was mama calling to tell me Myracle had called to say she and her sisters were going to stop by Easter Sunday to hang out. Mama was so excited.

She was glad to know the girls were accepting each other and us, as well.

MYRACLE

After I left the dinner at the Wilson's that night, I had so many thoughts racing through my head. It was so unbelievable. I had sisters and a brother, another uncle and grandmother, and enough money to pay for college. It was so unbelievable that the girl's life I saved, turned out to be my sister, and the cute guy my friends were trying to hook me up with at the movies turned out to be my brother.

I wondered what Grand D and Granny were going to say when I told them everything that had happened that night.

As I pulled into the driveway, Grand D was waiting on the front porch. "So how was it? How much are you going to get for college?" he asked, while eating a bowl of ice cream.

I sat down in the seat next to him and said, "It was nice. We had pork chops, fried chicken, mashed potatoes, green beans, cornbread and peach cobbler. Then we had Cookies and Cream ice cream and Double Stuff Oreo cookies."

"Those are your favorite foods," Grand D said.

"I know, but I didn't tell them that. It was good too. But don't tell Granny I said that. You know she doesn't like it when I say someone else's cooking is good," I whispered.

Grand D laughed, as Granny appeared in the doorway.

"What are you laughing about?" Granny asked, as she came out and sat in her rocking chair. "It feels good out here."

"I was just telling Myracle a funny story. That's all," Grand D said, as he winked his eye at me.

"How was the dinner?" Granny asked, rolling her eyes at Grand D.

"It was good," I replied, "we had pork chops, fried chicken, mashed potatoes, green beans, cornbread, and peach cobbler."

"I bet it wasn't as good as mine," Granny said.

I looked at Grand D. He smiled at me, and winked again. "Oh, of course not Granny. Nobody cooks like you."

"That's right. You're going to miss my cooking when you go away to college. Now, what did they tell you? How much money are you getting for school?" she asked as she rocked in her chair, which made a creaking noise every time she rocked backwards.

"Well, let me start from the beginning. The people who I met with were actually my father's mother and brother. My father died in November, and left money to the children he had, but never met before. I have a brother and two sisters, well, a brother and sister who are twins. And, my whole four years of college are going to be paid for. That girl I pulled from the burning car is actually my sister. Can you believe that?" I said. The looks on their faces told me they didn't know what to believe.

"Say that again," Grand D said, "but slower this time. I think I misheard what you said."

"No, Grand D. You heard me right."

"So this money is from your daddy, the one that your mother gave you the picture of for Christmas?" Granny asked.

I nodded. "Yes, and I saw that same picture in a photo album at the other grandmother's house."

Grand D looked at me. "I don't believe what I'm hearing. So that scholarship wasn't really a scholarship after all. It was a way for them to find you?"

"I guess so, but it is still a scholarship Mr. Wilson, my uh, uncle, calls a college fund, because it's paying for college. It's money we don't have to worry about anymore. When I graduate from college, the money I have left in the fund is mine."

"Well, it sounds like that was some dinner you went to. You left here at six o'clock an only child with one uncle and one set of grandparents, and came back with a whole 'nother set of relatives," Granny said.

"How do you feel about all of this, Myracle?" Grand D asked.

I thought about it for a few minutes and said, "I'm still the same person. I never met my father, although now I know his mother and his brother, who are very nice people. I am going to enjoy getting to know them, and I now know the two girls in school everybody kept saying

I looked like, are my sisters. I feel relieved I don't have to worry about how much college costs, and I can focus on the road ahead."

"You are a very mature young lady," Granny said.

"The other grandmother said she would like to meet you," I said, as I stood up to go inside.

"I'm sure we will be meeting real soon," Granny said, with an attitude.

As I walked in the house, I heard my grandfather say, "What's the problem?"

Granny replied, "No problem. None at all. I just don't like it that after all these years, these people show up, and want to be her family and pay for college. We're the one's who have taken care of this girl. Her own mama hardly does anything. Seemed like when that boy broke her heart, it messed up her mind too."

"Evidently, they just found out about the kids. And, they must be good people because they are trying to make up for what wasn't done in the past," Grand D replied.

"I don't like it. I still don't like it. And, I'm not going to like it! That's my baby in there, and I don't..." Granny didn't get to finish her statement. Grand D cut her off.

"You don't want to share her, that's what you don't want to do. I bet that other grandmother is a good woman, just like you. And if you had a grandchild somewhere out there in the world, you would try to find that child, and that's what she did. You would want to be apart of that child's life, just like she does. I wouldn't give up that baby in there for nothing in the world, and I'd go through hell and high water to get to her if I had to. Don't try to fight this. She needs our support right now, not our negativity. What you need to remember is that we have been her grandparents for eighteen years, so there's nothing this new grandparent can do to take our place." Grand D got up from his chair, gathered his ice cream bowl and spoon and headed inside the house.

"I hear what you're saying, but I still don't like it," Granny said, as she followed him inside.

The next morning, I overheard my grandparents in the kitchen telling Uncle Terry about the dinner. He was not thrilled about the fact that some strangers had invited me to their house and laid this news on me without them being there. I heard Uncle Terry saying he was going to have a talk with Uncle Martin. I knew the tone of his voice was angry sounding, and I didn't like it. My news was definitely unexpected, but I was happy to know I had sisters and a brother, and another uncle and grandmother.

My siblings and I had exchanged phone numbers and talked about getting together so we could get to know each other.

Everett would be back in town for Easter, so we decided to hang out then, and meet at Mama Wilson's house on Easter Sunday.

It was funny explaining to my friends I'd found out Serenity and Admire, who I now talked to everyday at school, were my sisters. I avoided going into details as much as possible.

My mother stopped by my grandparent's house one evening on her way to work. She had come into my room to give me something she'd bought me at the mall, and noticed the pictures on my dresser next to the one she'd given me of my father. She looked at them, then at me and said, "Where did these pictures come from Myracle? Who are these people?"

"Well, Mama, those are my father's other kids, and his mother and brother. I met them the day after my birthday. That scholarship I applied for was actually money from my father who died this past November."

"Isn't this the girl who was in the hospital, the one you saved from the burning car?" she asked, looking confused.

I nodded my head. "Yes, Admire. The other girl's name is Serenity and that's her twin, Everett. All of us have the same birthday, and we are all the same age."

"What? How is that possible?" my mother asked.

"I don't know, but it is."

"So, Laramie was a player I see," she said, with a smirk on her face. "Oh, well, may he rest in peace. You have to be careful when it comes to men. They can't be trusted."

"Well, maybe not. But, he felt bad about not being in our lives. See, read this." I handed my mother an envelope.

"What is it?" she asked.

"Just open it."

She opened the envelope, and took out the folded paper. She sat down on my bed, as she read the contents.

To the child of Alicia Lee:

If you are reading this letter, then my brother has done his job, and found you. My name is Laramie Mitchell Wilson, and I am your father.

I met your mother my senior year in high school. She was so beautiful, and funny. She was a cheerleader, and was also very smart. We had English together, and I always caught myself staring at her.

One day she noticed me staring at her, and she started blushing. After that, I tried to talk to her, but she gave me the cold shoulder. She said she didn't like jocks. She said that although I seemed smart, she believed most athletes had only two things on their mind, one being sports, and the other, well, sex.

And she was right. However, I was really just trying to get to know her, because I loved her smile and the way she laughed.

Finally after eight months of trying to get your mother to go out with me, she said yes. I had to pick her up from your grandparent's house, and meet your grandparent's and your uncle, because they were not going to allow me to just drive up and blow the horn for her to run outside.

After dating for two months, we got careless, and well, nine months later, you were born.

I am writing this letter to let you know that I apologize for any hurt I may have caused your mother after finding out she was pregnant. I was young then, and I am sure I could have handled things a little different. I was scared too, because I wasn't ready to be a father, and be responsible for a baby.

My mother never knew about the pregnancy, and didn't find out until she read the letter I wrote to her, which she didn't read until after I passed away.

I want you to know I have thought about your mother, and the hurt I must have caused her. I hope she hasn't wasted time the past seventeen years hating me, because I didn't deserve that much of her time. She was a very special young lady, and I hope she will find it in her heart to forgive me.

I was a good person. I mentored youth, and went to church on Sunday. I asked God to forgive me everyday for not taking care of the children I carelessly brought into this world.

I say children, because by the time you read this letter, you will find out that you have siblings. That doesn't mean that I cared for your mother any less than previously stated, it just means that I was irresponsible and I used poor judgment. I met three beautiful women who all had different personalities and characteristics I loved, and I didn't want to choose between the three. So, I split up my time and consequently, got them all pregnant.

Now, as my child, I wish you the best in having good sense of character and values, so you don't make the same poor choices like I did. I won't call you a mistake. I'm not calling any of you a mistake, because if you are here in this world, you are where God intended you to be, and He doesn't make mistakes.

Please accept my mother and brother as your family. Please make an effort to get along with your siblings, and love each other, because as my mother taught my brother and I as we were growing up, your family is your bloodline. Nobody is going to love you or appreciate you like family. Siblings need to get along, and love each other, no matter what. When it's all said and done, family will rush to the hospital to see about you and sit in the waiting room all night, pray for you when you can't pray for yourself, remember you on your birthday, remember your faults and laugh at your jokes and sit on the front row at your funeral.

When I found out I was dying, my brother was the first person I told, and the person who has stuck by me since that day.

Now, as my days are surely numbered, and I feel my life slipping away each day, I want you to know I have prayed for you, even though I never knew your name. I prayed for your health, for you to have sound mind and for you to be a good person.

I hope you accept my help in trying to make up for the times that I wasn't there to help care for you. I hope and pray you have a sense of direction, and that you have goals. I hope you want to do great things with your life, and I hope I can help you reach your goals by paying for your education.

Please accept my apologies for not meeting you in person, and for not being the father figure you probably hoped for.

My brother Martin is a wonderful, smart and hardworking man you can go to for anything.

Take care of yourself, and if you should have some situations in your life that seem too difficult to overcome, pray to God, because He is the one who is able to do all that you could ever hope or need for Him to do.

By now you already know what my favorite foods are, and my hobbies, but if you don't remember anything else about me, please remember the Bible verse I most related to throughout my life is Ecclesiastes 3:1-8: to every thing there is a season, and a time to every purpose under the heaven: a time to be born, and a time to die; a time to plant, and a time to pluck up that which is planted; a time to kill, and a time to heal; a time to break down, and a time to build up; a time to weep, and a time to laugh; a time to mourn, and a time to dance; a time to cast away stones, and a time to gather stones together; a time to embrace, and a time to refrain from embracing; a time to get, and a time to lose; a time to keep, and a time to cast away; a time to rend, and a time to sew; a time to keep silence, and a time to speak; a time to love, and a time to hate; a time of war, and a time of peace.

As you become an adult, remember the seasons, and remember to make a difference in someone else's life in a positive way. Don't spend time hating, because hate takes too much energy. Love as much as you can, because when you love, you get love in return.

Sincerely,

Your father,

Laramie Mitchell Wilson

My mother had tears streaming down her face, just as I had when I read the letter my uncle Martin mailed to me a few days before.

I handed her a tissue, and moved closer to her.

"He wasn't a bad guy," she said. "I just hated him for not taking responsibility for you."

"I know. But, now, at least you know he did think you were special. Like he said, you need to stop wasting your energy being angry at him for not being there all those years."

"I guess," she said, as she handed the letter to me, and got up to leave my room.

As she left, I opened the letter, and read it again. It was something I would always cherish, and someday share with my own children.

My siblings and I tried to spend time with each other each week. I visited Mama Wilson at least twice a week, because she lived closer to my house than she did the others.

As graduation grew closer, my siblings and I began to make plans to have one big graduation celebration, uniting all of our families.

I overheard my grandparents talking late one night, about three weeks before graduation. I had gone into the kitchen to get some Doritos. They were talking about some test results that had come back. Granny was crying. Grand D was telling her everything was going to be okay. He told her he loved her and reminded her they had been through many hard times together, and this one would be no different. There was a pause in the conversation. Then they began again.

"Do you think we should tell the kids?" Granny asked.

"Yes, we need to tell them. We shouldn't keep something like this from them," Grand D replied.

"What about Myracle? How do you think she'll take the news?"

Grand D sighed. "Myracle is a mature young lady. She will be able to handle this. I would rather her find out from us, than from someone else."

I couldn't wait to find out what they were talking about, and although I knew I wasn't supposed to be eavesdropping, I couldn't help but feel the need to burst into their room and ask them what they were talking about.

I heard Grand D tell Granny not to worry. I heard him tell her they could get a second opinion. I heard Granny tell him she didn't want a second opinion. She knew the doctor was right.

I could hardly sleep that night. The words cancer and death kept creeping into my thoughts. I prayed to God that night, just as I had every night, and asked Him to fix whatever it was my grandparents were dealing with at that moment.

At breakfast the next morning, I looked at Grand D as he read the newspaper, and I waited for Granny to sit down at the table after she placed the large stack of pancakes in front of me. I wondered if this was the right time to let them know I had overheard their conversation and wanted to know what was wrong and whom it was wrong with.

After Grand D led us in prayer, and we all fixed our plates with eggs, sausage and pancakes, Grand D started talking about the weather.

They were acting as if nothing was wrong, and I could hardly contain myself as I sat there pretending like there wasn't a secret I needed to be made aware of.

"I overheard the two of you talking last night when I came into the kitchen to get a snack. So, who's sick?" I blurted out.

My grandparents looked at me, then at each other.

Grand D placed his fork on his plate, took a long gulp of his orange juice, and said, "Well, we were going to wait and tell you when we told your mother and Terry, but since you overheard our conversation, I guess there's no sense in waiting. Your grandmother went to the doctor and he said she is in the beginning stages of Alzheimer's."

I looked at granny, and said, "Is that all? I thought somebody had cancer and was dying or something. Granny, don't worry, there are a lot of new medications now for Alzheimer's patients. We have been talking about it in my science class. Grand D was right. We do need to get a second opinion so we can find out the best treatment route for you. Don't worry. I will always be here to help you remember when you start to forget. And I won't let anyone put you in a nursing home either. Gammy's grandmother is in a nursing home, and she says that it's such a sad place. Gammy's grandmother has Alzheimer's, but they didn't catch the symptoms in time to try and start treating it before it got worse."

Grand D smiled. "You don't have to worry about the nursing home. I wouldn't dare send my *Sweet Thang* to a nursing home," he said, making Granny blush.

Knowing there were so many other ailments that could have been plaguing my grandparents, I was okay with the fact that Granny had been diagnosed with Alzheimer's. I knew eventually, the disease would rob her of memories of her past and her present, but I hoped by the time I finished college, someone would have found a cure which would allow her to remember me, her little Myracle.

MARTIN

About a week after the dinner, I began receiving phone calls from a man named Terry. My secretary had given me several messages, but each time I returned the phone call, I was unable to reach him.

After three weeks of playing phone tag, my secretary came into my office and told me there was a gentleman named Terry waiting to see me. I was anxious to find out who this guy was since he'd been calling me for three weeks leaving messages.

"Send him in. Did he make an appointment with you?" I asked her.

"No, he just showed up, and asked if you were here," she said, shrugging her shoulders, as she turned to escort him into my office.

I sat behind my desk, waiting for the man to enter my office, wondering if he was a potential client or a disgruntled witness I was interviewing for a case I was working on.

After a few minutes, a tall, thin, light skinned man with an unpleasant look on his bearded face walked into my office.

I stood as he entered, and extended my hand to shake his.

"Hello," I said. He shook my hand. "I'm Martin Wilson."

"Yeah. I know. I've heard a lot about you. I'm Terry Lee, Myracle Lee's uncle."

I was surprised to see him standing in my office. "It's nice to meet you. Please have a seat," I said, as I took my seat. "Can I offer you a drink? Coffee, water, a Pepsi?"

"No, thanks. I wanted to come by and talk to you about my niece, Myracle. And from what I understand, she's your niece too."

"Okay. She is a very smart young lady."

"Yes, she is. And she has always been a happy person. My parents and I have been her family. Your brother broke my sister's heart; so she chose not to spend a lot of time with Myracle. And I'm here because I don't want to see Myracle's heart get broken by you, and whatever this, this scholarship scheme you've come up with to get in her life after eighteen years."

I got up from my desk, and walked over to close the door to my office. I walked back around my desk, and sat down.

"I understand how you feel. I am an attorney, and a decent man, so I assure you I wouldn't do anything to hurt your niece. I'm not sure how much Myracle told you, but let me explain to you my side of this situation." I got up from my desk and went to the mini refrigerator in my office and got two bottles of water. I could tell this man was there out of the best interest for Myracle. I could understand how he was feeling, because I would probably feel and act the same if the tables were turned, and I had helped raise my niece for eighteen years, and some strangers show up claiming to be long lost family with money.

I handed him a bottle of water, and sat down behind my desk.

"I found out about your niece, and my brothers other children a few months before he died. He asked me to find his children, and that's what I did. There was no easy way to go about doing it, and I had concerns about someone getting hurt or being upset. But all of the kids seem to be just fine. My mother and I hoped this whole process would go smoothly, and that something positive would come from it. There is nothing shady about our presence in Myracle's, or the other kid's lives. I assure you everything is on the up and up. We plan to be a positive part of Myracle's life. I know I would have reservations about strangers showing up and claiming to have money for my niece from her long lost father. But we, my mother and I, want to be a part of her life, and be there for her in anyway we can. We can't make up for what my brother didn't do in the past, but we hope she will accept us as her family, just as you and your parents are her family."

"All that sounds cool, and everything, but why didn't you come talk to us, her family, first? Why didn't you check with us, to see if we were okay with this? Why didn't you invite us to the dinner so we could have been there when you broke the news to her."

"Honestly, it didn't have anything to do with you, or the other members of your family. It was really about finding my brother's children, and letting them know they had other family who wanted to be a part of their lives. But the most important thing I needed to do was let them know their father left them money to pay for their college education."

"I disagree with you. This had everything to do with my parents and me. We are the ones who have protected her all of her life. We are the ones who have raised her, took care of her when she was sick, and have been here to encourage her to become the outstanding young lady that she is. If this plan of yours had backfired, we, my parents and I, would have been the ones who would have had to comfort her, and try to make her understand. You are just lucky things turned out the way they did. I love Myracle, she is the only niece I have. I will do anything for her, and I will protect her from anything and anyone I believe will hurt her. Now, I'm not saying that you and your mother plan to hurt her, but I just had to come here to be sure that you and I understand each other. You seem like a nice, upstanding man. I asked around, and no one had anything bad to say about you, or your mother. So, I'm going to trust that you, just like I, have my niece's best interest at heart."

"Mr. Lee, I guarantee you that my mother and I only have Myracle's best interest at heart. This hasn't been easy for us. My parents taught my brother and I to be responsible growing up. When he got your sister, and those other girls pregnant, that wasn't something he was taught. My mother was not happy when she found out he had children somewhere that he had not taken care of."

"Well, I'm glad we could have this talk, man to man, because Myracle seems to really like you and your mother, and those other kids. I have always wanted the best for her, and I always will. I hope you can understand that," he said, as he stood up to leave.

I extended my hand to shake his, and said, "I understand. And now, that I am an uncle of three nieces and a nephew, I imagine that I will have a similar conversation at some point with someone about their best interest. So I appreciate you, and the way you have been such a good role model for Myracle. She talks about you a lot, and mentioned how you read to her when she was growing up, and how you taught her to drive. You have been an important part of her life. I don't want to take your place, I only hope I can in someway add to what you have already done for her."

Terry smiled at me, and shook my hand. "Well, thank you and I imagine I will be seeing you around. It was nice meeting you," he replied, as he headed towards the door.

"It was nice meeting you too," I told him as I walked behind him.

"My parents would like to meet you and your mother. They, well, we, are all real protective of Myracle. And she has been saying a lot of nice things about the two of you. So, whenever you get a chance, we need to make that happen," he said, as he walked out the door of my building.

"I will get with my mother, so we can arrange that meeting."

On the Friday after Easter Sunday, the police positively identified Stephanie's remains. However, they couldn't find any evidence to try and solve her case. They believed she had been dead since possibly Christmas night, the last time anyone saw her, but there were no clues in the vicinity of the crime scene to tell them what had happened.

It looked like Stephanie's death would become an unsolved mystery, which was never good for families.

Simone and her family were not surprised, but grief stricken nonetheless.

ADMIRE

I was totally shocked at the dinner. My mother and I had never really talked about my father. I had asked her a few times about him, and she told me small details like him being an athlete, and that they went to school together. She had told me his name was Mitchell, and that she had only seen him once after she found out she was pregnant.

When my mom picked me up that night, I was quiet on the ride home, but when we got in the house, I asked mom if I could talk to her in my room.

"Sure," she said, and followed me as I rolled myself down the hallway.

"Can you close the door, please," I asked her as we entered my room. "I want to talk to you about something probably best discussed between us first, before we include the other people in the house." That night, I had managed to get out of my wheelchair and onto my bed much quicker than I had been able to on other nights.

"Are you okay Admire," mom asked, noticing I seemed frustrated about something. "Did something happen at the dinner?"

"I'm okay. But I found out at the dinner I have a brother and two sisters. The dinner was hosted by my father's mother and his brother. My father died in November, but set up a college fund for all of his children. That girl, Myracle Lee, the one who pulled me from the car is my sister! It was my sister who saved my life. And do you know what else is eerie?"

"No, tell me," my mom said, as she sat on my bed looking at me, unsure of what to say.

"All four of us have the same birthday, and the three girls all have the same middle name, it's just spelled different. We all have the same favorite foods, Cookies and Cream ice cream, Cool Ranch Doritos and Double Stuff Oreo cookies. My father's mother, who we are going to call Mama Wilson, cooked my favorite meal tonight. Pork chops, fried chicken, mashed potatoes, green beans, cornbread and peach cobbler. Did you know I had siblings?"

"No, honestly after I told your father I was pregnant, I didn't hear from him again. I believe he was afraid, and at that point in my life, I needed someone to be there for me, and not be afraid of what the future held."

"Were you mad at him for not helping you with me?" I asked.

"I have to admit there were times when I got angry with him for not being there. I felt like he could have been more responsible. It's not all his fault, because I should have used protection, even if he didn't. But, things just kind of happened, and that's why I used to tell you if you ever got to the point where you found yourself in a situation where you might get pregnant, think first and react second. Don't get caught up in the moment, because one moment can have lifetime consequences. Now, I wouldn't trade you for anything in the world, but if I had been thinking that day, you wouldn't be here right now."

"They were all really nice. Serenity and Everett, who are twins, just found out during Christmas they are actually brother and sister, instead of cousins. That's so crazy."

My mom nodded her head. "Yes, I have to agree that is crazy."

"We took pictures, and decided we are going to start hanging out at school. So, I imagine that eventually they will come visit me here. Will you be okay with that?"

"Why wouldn't I be?" she asked.

"Well, because evidently, my father cheated on you with their mothers. I just thought that might make you angry."

"Admire, I am a happily married woman. I dated your father eighteen years ago. I am over him, and I certainly won't harbor a grudge against someone's children."

"Okay, I just wanted to make sure."

I was more determined now to walk. I did not want to be known as the crippled sibling. I wanted to spend time with my brother and sisters and new uncle and grandmother without that wheelchair hindering me. I started pushing myself harder in physical therapy.

About a week after the dinner, I got a letter in the mail. It was in a brown envelope, and when I opened it, I found pictures I had taken with my newly acquired family members, a picture of Laramie and another envelope addressed to the child of Valerie Moore.

I opened the envelope and pulled out the folded piece of paper. As I sat at the kitchen table, I read these words:

Dear Child:

If you are reading this letter, then my brother has located you. It was something that I had hoped to do myself, but failed to do after I learned that I was going to die.

My name is Laramie Mitchell Wilson. By now you have learned a little about me from my mother and brother. I am not sure if your mother ever told you anything about me, but I would like to share with you a piece of me, so you will know me.

I have always loved to read. I spent a lot of time, although I was an athlete, in the library. That is where I met your mother, Valerie. She walked in the library one day, and I thought I had seen an angel.

She saw me looking at her, and started laughing. After a few weeks, we talked on the phone, and she agreed to go to the movies with me one Sunday evening. After that, we went to the movies every Sunday.

We dated for four months, and then right before I got ready to leave for college, we broke up. I went to see her one more time, and that's when things happened.

I learned several months later that she was pregnant but I was immature and didn't know exactly what to do. So, I did nothing and tried to pretend she wasn't pregnant.

I apologize to you and to your mother for not being the man I should have been. I should have been there to help change your diapers, feed you, read to you and so much more.

I hope your mother has forgiven me, and I hope you too can forgive me for being absent from your life these past eighteen years.

Nothing can change the past, but it is my hope you and your siblings will get to know each other, along with my mother and brother.

I know you are thinking I was a player, since you and your siblings have the same birth date. But, I was young, and if I could change things, I would. But we can't change the past, so we have to try to make the future better.

That is why I have left a college fund for you. It is my hope that somehow you will forgive my past mistake, and find some good in me through the money I have left to pay for your college education.

I am not a bad person. I was just foolish and irresponsible a long time ago. As a grown man, I planned to find you and make things right. Then, I found out I was dying, and I didn't want to enter your life for a brief period of time, only to leave again.

My brother is a good man, who may not be your real father, but he can be there for you in my absence.

I want you to know I believe in God, and I volunteered my time to help with Hurricane Katrina victims. I gave freely to homeless people, although I didn't always believe that they were in need. But since it wasn't for me to judge, I shared with the homeless, as I believed God wanted me to. As the Bible says, to whom much is given, much is required. God had definitely blessed me with much, so I helped others as much as I could.

As I close, I want you to remember me for something positive. I want you to remember my favorite Bible passage is from the Book of Ecclesiastes, chapter 3, verses 1-8, and is the passage that talks about seasons. In your spare time, take a moment to look it up, because there is a very powerful message there for you.

When you eat a bowl of Cookies and Cream ice cream and some Double Stuff Oreo cookies, think of me, because they were my favorite kind of ice cream and the only kind of cookie I would eat. When you see a bag of Cool Ranch Doritos, think of me, and know I ate so many of them, it made me sick to my stomach.

When you hear a song on the radio or on your mp3

player by India Arie, think of me because she was one of my favorite artists. Her songs had a positive message for everyone.

When you watch a football game or read a book by Alice Walker, think of me because I loved football, and Walker was one of my favorite authors.

Do me a favor, and spend time with my mother. She is a wonderful woman, with so much to share. She's a great cook also, so in your spare time, visit her.

I apologize again for not being there for you. Please apologize to your mother for me, and ask her to forgive me, because life is too short to waste time being angry with people.

I want you to know that although I never knew your name, I prayed for you every day. I prayed for your health, and I prayed for your safety. I prayed God would watch over you and send you what you needed, in my absence.

I hope you find peace throughout your days. I pray God grants you the desires of your heart.

Take care, until we meet someday on the other side.

Your father,

Laramie Mitchell Wilson

I wiped the tears from my face, and read the letter again. I was unsure of what to think, or how to feel, but I was glad to know that as my father was waiting to die, he thought about me, even though he didn't know my name. And the fact he remembered my mother's name let me know he did care about her.

I tried not to feel sorry for myself, but I had missed the Cheerleading Competition my squad had won the past two years. My team invited me to go, but I was too upset about having to just watch, and not being able to participate. Lisa told me I was allowing the fact I couldn't walk to take over my spirit. She said I was letting my current dilemma control me.

"You're allowing this one thing to make you lose sight of other things. You could be dead, Admire. But you're very much alive," Lisa told me one day at school during lunch.

"That's easy for you to say. You're not the one in this wheel chair. You can walk and run, and turn flips until you get tired," I replied, upset she had pointed out my unpleasant disposition.

"Even if I couldn't, I don't think I'd be sitting around pouting about it. This is just one of the things you are good at. You haven't volunteered at the nursing home, or been singing in the choir at church. God didn't take away your voice. He just put a stop to your steps for the moment. What's wrong with you?"

"I don't know. When God took away my ability to walk, I guess a piece of my joy went away too. I know I should be thankful that I'm alive, and I am. But I just want to be normal again."

"You are normal. You're the same, normal Admire you were before the accident. Still funny, when you want to be, still pretty, smart, intelligent, and you're still a cheerleader, whether you are building pyramids or not. Once a cheerleader, always a cheerleader," Lisa said, with a smile.

My Uncle Vincent came by to see me one Saturday. He brought me some new books.

"Hey, pretty brown eyes," he said, as he sat beside me on the sofa.

"Hey Uncle," I replied, as I glared at an episode of Law and Order.

"Are you learning anything from this show that's going to help you when you become a lawyer?"

"I guess. I have already seen this episode. It seems like there's nothing new on television. That's why I read so much I guess."

"Yes. That's why I brought you this new book I found at the used book store today," he said, handing me a book by one of my favorite authors, Chester Himes, *Cotton Comes to Harlem.*

"Thanks Uncle. I really enjoy his detective stories. They are much different from some of the other detective stories I have read."

"Yeah, I read this one a while back, so I think you will enjoy it. I heard you met your real daddy's people. How do you feel about that?" he asked, as he got up and went into the kitchen to get something to drink.

I reached for an Oreo and opened it up so that I could eat the inside first. Then, I took a sip of milk, and replied, "It's alright. I definitely wasn't expecting to find out about him like this. Mama never really talked about him. My new grandmother and uncle are nice. And, so are my new brother and sisters. It's crazy. I have seen my siblings off and on almost all of my life at school, and now I'm finding out they are related to me."

"Did you like them before?" Uncle Vincent asked, reaching for one of my cookies.

"I didn't dislike them. We all just had different friends, and different interests. Myracle played volleyball, runs track and is in the drama club. I didn't like drama and wasn't into track or volleyball. And Serenity is in the band. I heard she's a great saxophone player. And I've read her articles. She is the editor of the school newspaper. She's really good. She wants to be a journalist. We are all just, different."

"Your mama told me Myracle was the one who saved your life. How did you feel when you found out she was your sister?"

I paused for a few minutes. "God knew her heart and knew she was the kind of person who wouldn't be afraid to help somebody in need, and I'm glad He put her at the post office that day so she could help me. I imagine we will always be close, because I will always be grateful to her for saving my life."

"Really, is that why I hear you've been sitting around moping for the past few weeks?"

I looked at him and said, "I don't think I've been moping. I'm just, I don't know, waiting for something to happen. I guess I'm waiting on God to answer my prayers because I sure have been sending up a lot of them. I mean, sure, I'll admit, I'm sad I can't walk, and I lost my first real boyfriend. I feel like I don't deserve this. I'm so young. And I want my life to be normal, Uncle Vincent. I want to walk, not roll around in that dumb wheel chair." I reached for another Oreo.

"I hear what you're saying, but I also hear what you aren't saying. You haven't said you are making something happen. You haven't said you are thankful to God for letting you live to see another day. You haven't said even though you can't walk, you are thankful you still have a brain that works, and you can talk and hear and see, and aren't a vegetable lying in a hospital bed, unable to do anything for yourself, including going to the bathroom. I haven't heard you say you are grateful you can still use that beautiful voice of yours to sing at church, or that you are grateful your face isn't all cut up by the shards of glass that somehow managed to miss your beautiful face when the windshield shattered from the crash." My uncle opened my eyes that day. He painted a picture for me that had not been painted by anyone else. He made me see I was feeling sorry for myself, and showed me how my situation could have been much worse.

"Uncle Vincent, do you remember when Meemaw found out she had cancer, and she said if the good Lord was ready to take her, she was ready to go?"

"Yes, Admire. I remember," he answered, looking at me with a serious look I hadn't seen before.

"I believe she meant that. But me, I don't have that assurance inside of me like Meemaw. I can't say that whatever God wants from me, I'm ready to do it. I'd be lying if I said if God wanted me to stay paralyzed and wheel chair bound for the rest of my life, that I would be okay with that. I don't want to be this way. Not even if it's His will for my life. So, it's just hard for me to live with this...this situation I'm in, and know that there's a possibility I may be this way for the rest of my life. I have to make myself believe this is only temporary. I want to believe I will walk again. I have to believe it, even if my body isn't cooperating with my thoughts."

"I hear what you're saying, little girl. But Meemaw has been around for a long time. And she has that kind of faith and trust in God a whole lot of people don't have. She has old time religion. She has always believed that whatever God's will was for her life was just fine for her. Have you ever seen her sad?"

I thought about it for a long time. "Only when Papa died, and when her brother died."

"That's because she is a special type of woman. Her spirit doesn't let her get sad. She just believes in taking everything to God. She prays about everything. And I do mean everything. And when we got the phone call that you had been in the accident, she fell to her knees in the middle of the kitchen floor, while she was in the middle of frying me some of that delicious, golden brown, crispy chicken, and prayed for you, Admire."

I started laughing. The image of Meemaw with flour on her hands dropping to the floor to pray for me made me smile.

"I'm serious!" Uncle Vincent said.

"I know you are," I said and smiled.

"Now, you may not have that same type of religion Meemaw has because she's seasoned. But you still have enough religion in you to fight your way out of this slump you are in. And that's what I expect to hear you are doing from now on." He looked at me, with his eyebrow raised. "Because I have this cute little yellow Honda Civic sitting in my backyard I am having fixed up for you, so you are going to have to get those legs working so you can take it for a spin."

I looked at him, as he dangled a single key on a keychain with a picture of a smiley face in the air.

A huge smile came across my face. "You bought a car for me?" I asked.

"Yes. I actually bought it for your birthday, but…well, it wasn't the right time to tell you. So, I figured you needed some help in the initiative department. When you start walking, the car will be parked outside this house for you to drive. No pressure, just incentive."

He tossed the key to me and smiled.

"If I could get up, I'd give you a hug, Uncle Vincent," I said. "This is so cool. I can't wait to sit behind the wheel of my own car."

"Well, one step at a time. First you walk, then you drive. And this time, try to avoid the big trucks! Okay. The bigger the truck, the more damage. Try to remember that."

"I learned my lesson. Believe me. I will pay attention whenever I get to drive again. There was this annoying song that came on the radio, and I only looked down for a second, and then…"

My uncle nodded his head. "I know, it only takes a second. That's how my first accident happened. So, keep your eyes on the road."

After my uncle left that day, I felt a little better. And in the days that followed his visit, I started seeing changes.

I started taking small steps on my own, after I realized the feeling was coming back in my legs. I didn't tell anyone because I wanted to know for sure that the change we had all been praying for was happening.

I would try to walk in my room at night when everyone else was asleep, and each time I tried, my spirits were lifted because I was getting stronger and stronger.

Around the middle of May, I found out I was definitely the valedictorian of my senior class. I was excited because I knew I was going to walk across the stage on graduation day, and I was going to stand on my own two feet behind the podium and deliver my speech.

I was surprised to find out that my sister, Myracle, was graduating number two in my class. How crazy was that. My sister and I would be sitting beside each other on the stage at graduation ceremony.

MAMA

I was on my way to prayer meeting three weeks after the dinner. I was running late because I had decided at the last minute to go. I hadn't made a prayer meeting service since Laramie died. I didn't feel up to going. However, with everything seeming to come together, I felt as though a weight had been lifted from my shoulder.

As I grabbed my keys from the counter, the front doorbell rang.

I looked out the window, and saw a dark blue SUV. I didn't know anybody who drove an SUV, so I was hesitant about going to the door. My car was parked in the garage, so I could pretend I wasn't home.

The doorbell rang again. I looked through the peephole but didn't recognize the lady standing on the other side of the door. She didn't look like she was trying to sell me anything, so I opened the door.

"Hello. May I help you?" I asked, looking at her through the screen.

The lady was very pretty, and well dressed.

"Are you Mrs. Wilson?" she asked.

"Yes."

"My name is Valerie. I'm Admire's mother."

I opened the screen door. "Please, come in," I said. "It's nice to meet you."

"It's nice to finally meet you too," she replied.

I motioned for her to have a seat. I observed her looking around my living room, and I saw the look on her face as her eyes fell on the picture of Laramie on the fireplace. She sat down on the sofa, and I sat down next to her.

"I won't take up much of your time," she said, looking nervous. "I just wanted to…well, I wanted to talk with you about my daughter."

"Ok, dear. Can I offer you something to drink, some tea, coffee?" I asked, getting up to go to the kitchen.

"Some water is fine," she said.

When I came back into the living room, I saw her flipping through the photo album on the coffee table.

"Admire is a very sweet and beautiful young lady," I said, as I handed her a bottle of water. "She's very intelligent too. You have done a wonderful job raising her. I must say I am glad you stopped by today. I was looking forward to meeting you."

"Thank you Mrs. Wilson. The past few months haven't been easy. The accident has taken away most of Admire's joy. She was so excited the day she came home telling me about the scholarship she was going to apply for. She was stressing about the essay, hoping she wasn't too personal. Then, she took forever, selecting just the right photo to send with it." She turned her face towards the bookshelf, where Admire's picture sat in a frame between Serenity and Myracle's. "When she came home after the dinner that night, she had a lot of questions for me. We had never really talked about her father. When she was younger, she'd ask about him, but as she got older, she consumed her spare time with friends, and cheerleading and books, so the subject never came up again. Imagine how surprised I was when she came home that night and told me she had met her father's mother and brother, along with her father's three other children."

She paused for a few minutes, looked at Laramie's picture again, then began speaking. "I can't say I'm not grateful for her education being paid for. To be honest, I wasn't worried about it because I have been saving for her college expenses since I started teaching. And since she is graduating at the top of her class, she has several other scholarships to help pay for some of her expenses. She seems to be excited about finding out about you, and her new uncle, and brother and sisters. However, I am not at all happy about the way this whole thing happened. I feel like I had the right to know about you, and Laramie's death. I am her mother. I feel like I should have been consulted before you and your son told her about...all of this..." she was getting upset.

I touched her arm softly, and said, "Let me apologize to you for not contacting you personally. Laramie left instructions with his brother to find Admire and the other children. Martin felt that the easiest way to go about it was to just deal with the children. I don't think that either of us intended to slight the mothers, and I'm sorry if that has happened. When I first found out Laramie had fathered children and hadn't told me about them, let alone taken care of, I was so angry with him. I didn't find out until after his funeral. And, I found out through the letter he wrote me, but didn't want me to read until after he was gone. I want you to know I didn't raise Laramie to be irresponsible. My husband and I instilled morals and values into both of our sons. However, I've learned it isn't the fact that children aren't given the necessary tools to become responsible, upstanding adults, it's that they don't always use them. As a mother, I understand how you feel, seeing as how two strangers have come into your daughter's life, after you have spent the past eighteen years molding and shaping her into an amazing young woman. But, we are here to add to her life. We are her family too, and just like you, we only want the best for her.

"When I read about her accident in the newspaper, I had heart palpitations. I prayed for her, not knowing her condition, but I prayed nonetheless. And, I have been praying for her since. I pray God allows her to walk again, because I know that's what she wants more than anything right now. I pray she finds peace in her heart and is able to wait patiently on God to work a mighty work in her life. Someone said that it takes only a few minutes to know you love someone. From the moment I found out I had grandchildren I knew I loved them. When I met them, I understood why. You are a beautiful woman. I applaud you for the sacrifices you have made over the years, and I am happy to know that God blessed Admire with the mother she needed, and not necessarily the mother she hopes to have when you fuss at her. If no one has ever told you, you have done an amazing job as a single mother, who has raised an amazing young woman." I squeezed her hand, as tears began to form in her eyes.

"Thank you," she said. She tried to hold back the tears, but they fell anyway. "Thank you very much." I handed her a tissue, and watched a mother release whatever frustrations she had been holding on to.

We spent the next hour talking. I showed her pictures of Laramie and Martin, and showed her the house. When she walked into Laramie's room, she was immediately drawn to a picture lodged in the top right hand corner of his dresser mirror. I had never paid much attention to it, although I'd seen it a thousand times. She walked over to the dresser, reached for the picture and said, "This was the picture we took the summer before he went away to college. We'd gone to Six Flags one Saturday, and took pictures in one of those booths. I can't believe he saved it, after all these years." She smiled, as another set of tears began to roll down her cheeks. She placed the picture back where she'd found it, and wiped the tears from her face.

"My son wasn't a bad person," I told her, as she looked at me. "He just made poor choices."

"Yes ma'am. I know."

We went back into the kitchen, and talked some more over a slice of cake and coffee.

"Admire said you were a great cook."

I blushed. "I don't know about great, but I do love to cook, and my husband and my sons loved to eat," I replied.

"How did you meet your husband?"

"At the library," I said with a smile.

"The library?"

"Yes. I was in college studying to be a teacher, and so was he. I spent a lot of time at the library, and one day, our eyes met, and well, that's the beginning of us. He was a really good man. I miss him, although he's been gone for over twenty-five years. He would have loved the grandchildren."

When Valerie left that night, almost four hours after she rang my doorbell, I felt as though I had gained a new friend. That was positive, because I knew so many grandparents who didn't get along with their grandchildren's mothers, especially when the child's parents weren't married.

SERENITY

My head began to hurt. So did my stomach. My aunt's boyfriend was standing in front of us saying he was my uncle and these girls were my sisters. I couldn't believe it. Life was springing one surprise after another on me. I felt like I was on a roller coaster, and every time it stopped moving, another family secret invaded my space.

The fact that my biological father had left me money to pay for college was good, since I had actually considered not going after my aunt passed away. But knowing I could go for free made me rethink my plans.

Aunt Simone followed Everett and I back to Nana's house after the dinner.

When we got there, a police car was leaving. When we entered Nana's house, she was crying.

"What's wrong?" I asked, walking over to the big comfy blue chair she was sitting in. I squatted down beside her and placed my hand on her arm.

"Nothing Baby. There's still no news about Stephanie. I hope they find her soon," Nana said, as she wiped her face with the back of her hand.

"I hope so, too," Simone added, as she sat on the sofa facing Nana.

"Well, now, that's enough sad talk, let's hear some good stuff. How was the dinner?" Nana asked, changing her posture to show her interest in what we had to say.

I looked at Everett who had made himself a seat on the floor next to Aunt Sarah. "Well, I don't think y'all are going to believe what we have to tell you. First of all," I continued, "Everett and I both have a college fund set up in our names. So, we don't have to worry about money for college."

Aunt Sarah looked at me, and then at Everett. "What in the world? How is that possible?"

Everett smiled and said, "Well, as it turns out, the dinner we went to was being hosted by our real daddy's mother and brother. And, we also found out we have two sisters. They were at the dinner too."

"Yeah, and we found out just in time because Everett was about to hook up with his own sister!" I said, teasing my brother.

Nana looked at Everett. "O, my Lord! Well, I should say, the Lord had a hand in this. 'Cause who would have thought of all the girls in this town, you'd be trying to make a connection with your sister. That's why children need to know who they are kin to."

Everett smiled, and Aunt Sarah shook her head in disbelief.

"What are your sisters like?" Nana asked, readjusting herself in the chair.

"They look just like us. Their names are Myracle and Admire," Everett said.

"Lord, have mercy. People sho' do come up with unusual names these days," Nana said, shaking her head in disapproval.

"And, we all have the same middle name, we just spell it different," I added.

"What's really interesting, is that Myracle saved Admire's life, and Serenity was there when it happened," Simone added. "If that's not divine intervention, I don't know what is."

"When did all of this happen?" Aunt Sarah asked.

"Just before Christmas," I answered. "I was on my way to mail my essay for the scholarship, and I saw a car accident. Myracle pulled Admire out of a burning car before it blew up."

"That's so amazing," Nana said.

"What's even more amazing is we were all at the post office on the same day mailing off the essays for this scholarship, which we found out tonight was really a college fund from the father none of us ever met."

"Well, I guess you have had an interesting evening," Aunt Sarah said, as she got up from the love seat.

"Yes, I would have to agree this evening has been quite interesting," I replied.

A few weeks after the dinner, I came home from school and found a letter in the mail addressed to me from my Uncle Martin. There was a white envelope inside the brown envelope, along with several pictures. One was the group picture we took at the dinner. As I sat down at the kitchen counter, I unfolded the letter and began to read it.

To the Child of Stephanie Bell:

First, allow me to apologize for never meeting you in person. I haven't always made the best choices in life, so I am choosing now to write this letter and share with you a little information about myself.

I'm sure by now you have heard I was a football player in high school, and a high school coach. I loved to read, and I loved to help people.

The summer I graduated from high school, I met Stephanie at a party. She was a very beautiful young woman, and I had hoped to keep in touch with her while I was away at college. That evening, as we sat in my car listening to music by the lake, she told me that sometimes she got depressed, and she couldn't understand why. She said she had thought about committing suicide from time to time and she said she had never told anyone. But for some reason, she felt she needed to get it off of her chest. I felt bad for her, and I wanted to try and be there for her; to encourage her if I could. Anyway, one thing led to another, and, four months later she wrote me a letter telling me she was pregnant.

I was not ready to be a father, I am sorry to admit. I have regretted my irresponsible actions on many occasions. It was not out of disrespect for your mother, I just honestly was not ready to be a father. I had big plans, and a baby wasn't one of them.

As I grew older, and wiser, I realized I had made a big mistake by not owning up to my actions. I had gotten three young ladies pregnant, and that wasn't something I was proud of. It wasn't something I could tell my mother either, because she didn't raise me to be irresponsible.

Sometimes, God has to put us on our back so that we can look up and see our shortcomings. He gives us ample opportunities to look back at the things we have done to hurt others, and significant opportunities to make amends.

I cannot change the past, but I hope I can help make the future better for you. I want you to think of positive things when you think of me, and not the negative fact that I wasn't there for you or your mother when you were growing up.

A few months before I found out I had cancer, a friend of mine told me he had seen some students at the high school that looked like they could be my children. He didn't give me their names, but said that the students were the spitting image of me. I had planned to try and find you, and my other children, but felt it wasn't a good idea to come into your life for a brief period of time, only to have death take me away.

I asked my brother to locate you, and to be there for you in my absence. My mother has always wanted grandchildren, so please get to know her, and spend time with her.

Please tell your mother I am sorry for any pain I may have caused her. I loved her, in my own way. I loved the corny jokes she used to tell, and the way she painted her toe nails different colors. I loved the sound of her voice when she sang like Whitney Houston, and I admired her courage in dealing with her issues of depression after we met.

I want to encourage you to dream big. You have my blood running through your veins, so I know you are very smart. Be the best at whatever you are hoping to be in life, and don't let anyone or anything break you down. Love yourself, even if no one else does. Learn to laugh at yourself, so when other people laugh at you, it won't bother you as much. Think first, then react, and think first, then speak. Because once words are spoken, they can never be taken back.

Make friends with your siblings, and respect each

other. Family is important and should stick together, regardless of what other people are saying or doing.

My father used to make me reread books if I couldn't tell him what I got out of them. He said every book had a point, and if you didn't get the point, then you hadn't gotten your monies worth.

I hope you get something out of this letter, and if you don't I pray you read it again so you take something positive from it, and carry it in your heart, the place where love grows.

Although I never knew your name, I prayed for you everyday. I prayed for God to bless you with good health, and I prayed for God to keep you safe from all hurt, harm and danger.

Something you may find strange about me, because most people have, is I eat ketchup on everything except Cookies and Cream ice cream and Double Stuff Oreo cookies. I even eat ketchup with my Cool Ranch Doritos.

I used to pretend like I was Ralph Tresvant from New Edition, and I'd sing in the mirror. Of course, I didn't sound like him, but I tried. Growing up, I missed my father so much after he passed away. I used to sit in his favorite chair just so I could feel his presence.

I have attended church faithfully all of my life. I know that God is going to take care of you, and your siblings, and I have faith enough to believe blessings are coming your way.

When you think of me, think positive thoughts. And laugh when you see a bottle of ketchup.

Until we meet, on the other side,
Your father,
Laramie Mitchell Wilson

I cried as I read the letter. I read it over and over again because I wanted to be sure I didn't miss the point. I looked at the picture of my father that had been included with the letter. I couldn't believe I was looking into the eyes of the person who helped create me.

I was upset with him for not being there for Stephanie. If he had been, maybe she would have been different. Maybe she wouldn't have started using drugs, and maybe she would have been a good mother to my brother and me.

In his letter he said he couldn't change the past, but he was hoping to make the future better for me. I hoped things were going to get better because the past few years for me had been hard.

It seemed as if my family had quite a bit of drama and sadness surrounding us my senior year.

A week after Easter Sunday, police identified the body they'd found behind the bus station as Stephanie, my birth mother. I felt like I was being punished, because I had already lost my adopted mother, then I found out my real father had died of cancer, and my real mother had been murdered. I was losing relatives, and getting new ones simultaneously.

Nana took the news about Stephanie the hardest. She had lost two children in two months. She was having such a hard time handling the news she had to be taken to the hospital because she was having chest pains.

She wanted to know who killed her baby. She asked God why did he take her. She was distraught because she kept saying it was her fault that something happened to her because she made her leave Christmas night after they had argued.

No one was able to calm her down, so the doctors had to give her some medicine.

My new family called to check on me after they found out my mother's body had been found. Mama Wilson came by Nana's house with a cake, and Uncle Martin stopped by to talk to Simone. I noticed she was wearing a really big rock on her finger that wasn't there the night of the dinner.

Stephanie's funeral was sad, but I felt really special when I turned around at some point during the funeral and saw Myracle and Admire sitting a few rows behind me. Admire was wiping her eyes, and Myracle looked as if she was trying to keep from crying.

Stephanie had always been the main source of drama in our family. Aunt Sheryl said Papi spoiled her because she was the baby.

As I sat there thinking about the last conversation I had with Stephanie,

I recalled her asking me was I embarrassed of her. I have to admit I was, and had always been embarrassed for people to know she was my mother. If it wasn't for the drugs, I wouldn't have been, but drugs make people do crazy things.

I realized I would never get to tell her what my father wrote in the letter, and she wouldn't bring her drama to any more family gatherings.

I cried only after I saw how much Nana was hurting. My tears were for Nana, not Stephanie.

MARTIN

It didn't seem right, Simone and I getting married so soon after her sister's funeral. But that's what she wanted. I told her we could move the date, but she said Saturday, May 12 was the date we'd set, and that's the date we were going to stick with.

Simone was a beautiful bride, and had asked Myracle, Admire and Serenity to be her bridesmaids. Her nephew, Everett, escorted her down the aisle.

Mama was excited we were finally getting married.

We had a small wedding at the church with immediate family and closest friends and a small reception at Mama's house.

We planned to take a cruise to Hawaii for our honeymoon after the kids' graduation.

I had a talk with Everett at the reception. Since I hadn't gotten the chance to learn much about him through an essay the way I had gotten to know the girls, I felt the need to learn more about him.

We were outside, in the backyard, watching family and friends talk and laugh. I hadn't seen mama laugh that much in a long time.

I saw Everett sitting in a corner, alone, with his headphones on, eating from a plate of meatballs, chicken wings, potato salad, grapes and strawberries. He looked a lot like Laramie, as he sat there.

"Mind if I join you?" I asked him, as I walked over with my own plate of food. "I'm starving."

"Me too. I love potato salad," he said, as he removed his headphones from his ears. He took another bite then took a gulp of his drink. I noticed

170

an extra plate sitting next to him piled high with Oreos, wedding cake and mixed nuts. He was definitely not shy when it came to food, and I was glad to see he felt comfortable enough to enjoy himself.

"So, tell me, Everett, what do you plan to study when you go to college?" I was enjoying mama's potato salad too. The chicken wings weren't bad either, but I wished the pieces were bigger. I was going to have to go back for seconds, maybe even thirds in order to get full.

He finished chewing his food and said, "Well, I've been thinking about it for a long time, and I've decided I want to study Forensic Science. I want to be a crime scene investigator. I like watching television series that show how investigators take bits and pieces and put them together to solve a crime. I think it's pretty cool."

I laughed. "Yes, it does look interesting on TV. But it's a lot more complicated in real life. It is an interesting field. I wish you much success with it. What made you decide to go to college all the way in Washington, D.C.?"

"Well," he said, after taking a bite of his second Oreo cookie, "I did a lot of research and found out George Washington University has a good Forensic Science program. I'll be able to get my Master's in crime scene investigation. I plan to study hard, especially since I have been given such a great opportunity. I really appreciate this college fund your brother left for me. I have other scholarship money coming to me, so I will be able to focus on studying and not have to worry about how I'm going to pay for my education."

"Sounds like you have a plan. How does your family feel about you going so far away from home?" I asked.

"Well, my mama thinks it's too far away, but my dad thinks it's a good idea, so I can become more independent. He said it will make a better man out of me, teach me how to make it away from home and learn how to get along with all kinds of people."

"Your dad sounds like a good man."

"He is. He's always been easy to talk to. He works a lot, so he hardly ever comes down when mama and I come. He is a police detective, so he rarely ever takes off. Mama says his job is going to kill him. How do you like your job, Uncle?"

No one had ever asked me that question before, so I was surprised when he asked me. "Well, I love my job. I have known since I was a kid I wanted to be a lawyer. At first it was because I liked the fact I could wear nice suits everyday and make a lot of money. But as I got older, it became more about me helping people, and making a difference in society. I feel good about myself when I help others, so I can't imagine myself doing anything else. How do you feel about everything that has been going on lately, with your birth mother, finding out Serenity is your twin, and finding out about my brother, and the extended family you have recently acquired?"

"It's all good," he replied. "This cake is the bomb. I didn't really have a lot to do with Stephanie, so no love lost there. I love Serenity, we've always been close, so finding out she's my sister rather than just my cousin is cool. I don't really know what to think about your brother, but the extended family is cool. Is this the house you grew up in?"

"Yes. My father was really proud of this house. He was the first person in his family to own such a nice home."

Everett nodded his head. "Have you read all those books on the shelves in the living room?"

I laughed. "Well, I have probably read most of them. Some of them were Laramie's. We liked different types of books. Did you play sports in school?"

"Yes Sir. I played baseball, and I am a member of a boxing club."

"Boxing? You don't seem like a boxer."

He smiled. "Yeah, I know. I do it to stay in shape, and the girls think it's cool. I'm pretty good at it. I've won some competitions. Mama doesn't like it, but my dad enjoys watching me compete."

"I'm just curious, but do you plan to cut your braids before you go to college? Sometimes people make the wrong impression by looking at you rather than getting to know you," I said, hoping not to offend him.

He smiled. "My parents told me the same thing. Mama wasn't thrilled when I came home with a tattoo on my arm either." He patted his right arm, showing me the area where the tattoo was hidden underneath his dress shirt. "My dad laughed when I came home and showed it to him."

"A tattoo? Wow. I never would have guessed," I replied. "What made you get a tattoo?"

"The guys in my boxing club all have one. We got them to show we were a team. But, to answer your question, I do plan to cut my braids off before I leave for college. I don't want to be judged by my looks. I've found people are surprised by how intelligent I am once they get to know me. It's been my experience people underestimate me. Some people think I'm a thug because I have braids. Some think I'm a pushover because I don't talk much. A few people, however, have had the opportunity to meet my dark side, which doesn't come out often."

"Well, if there's anything you need, let me know. If I can help you in any way, please ask. You seem like you have your head on straight. You seem like you have some direction. Just stay focused. Your parents have evidently taught you a lot to help you stay on the right track. I'm looking forward to visiting you on your job someday."

He smiled at me, and said, "The woods are lovely, dark and deep, but I have promises to keep. And miles to go before I sleep. And miles to go before I sleep."

I smiled back. "Robert Frost," I said as I laughed. "I agree. You have a long way to go before you finish."

I was impressed. I didn't expect Everett to recite poetry to me. My brother had managed to help create four very talented and intelligent children.

ADMIRE

On graduation day, Saturday, June 2, I surprised my family and friends when I refused to use the ramp for my wheel chair to get up on the stage. Instead, I slowly got up from the wheel chair, held on to the rail and walked up the steps like the other members of the senior class of 2007.

I set next to Myracle, who sat in front of Serenity, who had been asked to lead the Pledge of Allegiance.

Mama Wilson proudly sat next to Uncle Martin and his new wife. My mother and the other family members were sprinkled throughout the crowd. I could see Serenity's family all sitting together, and I saw Myracle's grandmother talking to Serenity's Uncle Thomas. Myracle's Uncle Terry was taking pictures. My Uncle Vincent was sitting over to the side with his camcorder video taping everything. He winked his eye at me when I looked in his direction and made me smile. As I looked from face to face of the people who had come to watch us take the next step into adulthood, I began to get nervous about making my speech.

As the time came for me to stand and deliver my thoughts to the senior class of 2007, I wondered if it had been a good idea after all for me to stand at the podium without any assistance or aid from my wheel chair.

Myracle and Serenity must have been watching me closely because just as my knees were about to buckle, they both rushed to my side, and each grabbed an arm to act as my crutches.

As tears formed in my eyes, I looked at Myracle on my right, and then at Serenity on my left. I never would have imagined that two girls I passed in the hallway of my school everyday for almost four years, and never said a word to, would end up standing beside me as my sisters while I gave my Valedictorian address.

I would forever be grateful to Myracle for saving my life, but I was also grateful to Serenity for speaking words of encouragement to me when no one was around. She was the one who told me to practice walking in my room when no one was looking and to take my physical therapy into my own hands. She was the one who reminded me to speak life into my situation and believe that I could walk. She was also the one who told me no one could feel sorry for me, if I didn't give them a reason to.

The next day, a caravan of cars headed to Everett's graduation ceremony two and a half hours away.

I was planning to be one hundred percent recovered by the first day of my college classes. I planned to drive myself in the car my Uncle Vincent had given me.

EVERETT

I was definitely surprised to know I was getting money to pay for college left for me by my biological father, I never knew existed.

It was strange finding out Serenity was my twin sister, and not my cousin, as I had been led to believe all of my life.

It was disheartening the way Stephanie's words cut through my heart that Christmas night. I won't ever forget the look on her face, or Serenity's when she dropped not one, but two bomb shells on me.

I had no idea that I was adopted. Sarah was my mother as far as I was concerned, and Will was my father. The two of them raised me, and taught me right from wrong, about the Word of God, about respect and responsibility. Stephanie would never be my mother, regardless of what she said.

I was glad to learn Serenity was my sister. I had always felt a connection with her I felt with no one else. I was sick for weeks when we moved away a few years ago because I missed her so much. We were like best friends.

I guess things have a way of working out. I have enough money to go to college, and I don't have to worry about Stephanie trying to embarrass me by telling people she is my birth mother.

Some family secrets should stay a secret, and the one about Stephanie giving birth to me is one that should have been kept. I love knowing I have a sister, but I could have done without Stephanie's baggage that came with the news.

I used to feel sorry for Serenity after I learned at an early age that Aunt Sheryl and Uncle Thomas had adopted her when Stephanie was sixteen. I was glad no one would have to know my birth mother was addicted to drugs and sold herself to get a fix. I was glad as far as anyone knew Stephanie was just my crack head aunt.

That Christmas night, after Stephanie blurted out she was my mother and declared Serenity and I were twins, I felt sick to my stomach. I was overwhelmed by shame and embarrassment. I couldn't stand the thought of having to tell anyone Stephanie was my birth mother.

I had a flashback to when I was about five years old. I was at Nana's house on Easter Sunday. I had gone into the restroom to wash my hands after getting chocolate on them. Stephanie came into the restroom, and closed the door behind her.

She came over to me, and told me I looked just like my daddy. She told me one day she would tell me a secret when I was old enough to understand. She told me Sarah was just the caregiver, but she had been the life giver.

I didn't understand what she meant by that then. But, when I thought back on that conversation, I understood.

I had gone outside to get some fresh air after Serenity left Nana's house that Christmas night with Aunt Sheryl and Uncle Thomas. Stephanie must have been really high because I could still hear her arguing with Nana as I stood by the window of Nana's bedroom, which was just off the back porch. I heard sounds of a struggle, and then Nana slapped Stephanie, and Stephanie slapped Nana back.

I couldn't believe what I was hearing. I was boiling inside because Stephanie had the nerve to hit Nana! I heard my mother and father, Sarah and Will, go into the room and try to defuse the situation. Things were way out of control.

I heard Nana tell Stephanie to get out of her house, and not to come back until she got herself together.

I heard Stephanie tell Nana if the family hadn't made her give up her babies, she might not have ended up the way she was.

I heard Sarah saying it was for her own good they took the twins because Stephanie was too young and irresponsible to raise us.

I heard Stephanie tell Sarah she would have been a good mother, but no one gave her the chance.

When Stephanie ran out of the house just before eight o'clock that night, and walked down the street towards the bus stop, I followed her.

She must have heard my footsteps behind her, because she turned around.

"What are you doing out her?" she asked, with black eyeliner stains on her face. She looked like trash, with her hair all over the place, her makeup a mess and her clothes disheveled. She looked exactly how I pictured a crack head, and not someone's mother.

"I wanted to talk to you about what happened back there," I told her as we walked over to the bench at the bus stop and sat down. "Why did you choose tonight to tell me you are my birth mother, and Serenity is my twin?"

She looked at me, tilted her head to the side and said, "I told you along time ago I had a secret to tell you. And, I thought it was time to let you know the secret. You are a man now. Seventeen years old. Haven't you ever wondered why you don't look like Sarah and Will? Didn't you ever notice how much you looked like Serenity?" She pulled her jacket tighter because the wind was blowing, and snow flurries were starting to fall. I should have brought a heavier jacket, but in the rush, I wasn't thinking about the weather. I was glad I'd grabbed my gloves.

"I only thought about it when other people brought it up. Sarah and Will are the only parents I have ever known, and whom I will always consider my mother and father. That scene you caused back there, getting Serenity and Nana, and everybody else all excited, doesn't bother me. I always knew you were evil and crazy. Everyone tried to say it was the drugs making you do dumb stuff to make Nana and the rest of the family worry about you. But, deep down, I just believe you are the rotten apple of the family. If Sarah and Will hadn't taken me, and Sheryl and Thomas hadn't taken Serenity, we would have been raised by foster parents anyway. CPS would have taken us from you because there's no way you would have been a good parent." I looked down the street. The bus wasn't coming. I heard a noise behind me, and turned to see a dog trying to get into the trashcan behind the bench.

She turned to look me in my eyes and said, "You sound like you hate me Everett. You don't even know me. You don't know what I've been through these past few years. You act like you all that. You are my child! I carried you under my heart for eight and a half months! I gave birth to you! I am your mother! And there's nothing you can do to change that! You hear me? Nothing! So get used to it!" she yelled at me, and got up from the bench. She was pacing back and forth, and looking down the street for the bus.

"You will never be my mother," I said, with a tone of hatred that seemed to have stirred up in me from deep down inside. "You may have carried me, but Sarah and Will are my parents. You have never been to a school play, signed a report card, stayed up with me all night when I was sick, helped me with my homework, come to the school to talk to a teacher on my behalf, took a picture of me on the first day of school, bought me a birthday present or a Christmas present, cooked me dinner, ironed my clothes or told me a Bible story. You have never read me a book, tied my shoes, run my bath water, put a band-aid on my knee, fussed at me for not cleaning my room, cheered for me at a baseball game or shared a piece of family history with me. That was what Sarah and Will did! They are my parents! NOT YOU!" I yelled back as I got up from the bench.

Stephanie walked over to me and slapped my face so hard I stumbled a little as the taste of blood formed in my mouth. She was shouting something at me, but I couldn't hear what she was saying.

I was so mad all I could think to do was slap her back. She didn't mean anything to me. She was just a crack head. Before I knew it, I hit her hard enough to make her fall down and bang her head against the edge of the bench, causing it to bleed immediately. She didn't get up. I waited a few minutes. She just lay there, bleeding. I called her name; she didn't respond. I walked over to her, and realized she was dead.

I started to panic. I didn't know what to do. I didn't mean to kill her. I just wanted her to shut up and go away.

Shut up.

Go away.

I shut her up, and now I could make her go…away.

I looked around, and there was no one in sight. I had to figure out what to do. I thought about just leaving her there, but changed my mind because I knew Nana would be devastated if the police showed up at her door with the news they had found Stephanie's body.

I had to think. I remember pacing back and forth. I had never been in a situation like that before. So I didn't know what to do. The snow was beginning to come down harder. I couldn't think of any other solution, so I drug her body to the field behind the bus stop, covered it up with some trash I found lying around and prayed God would forgive me, as I ran back to Nana's house. It was a good thing I was wearing my gloves. There would be no fingerprints to lead the police back to me if they ever found her body.

I received a letter in the mail my father apparently wrote before he died. There were some pictures of us that were taken at the dinner that night, and a picture of my father. I unfolded the letter, which was addressed to the child of Stephanie Bell. However, when I saw her name at the top of the page, I folded the letter and placed it back in the envelope. I'd read it eventually, at some point when I could stand the thought of someone addressing me as the child of Stephanie. As far as I was concerned, Sarah had always been, and would always be my mother.

Family secrets can be devastating.
Some are best kept a secret.
I pray my secret stays between me, and God.

READ IT AGAIN, PLEASE!

A FEW MORE FAVORITES...

BECAUSE MY MOTHER WAS MEAN

My mother was so mean when I was growing up. *Or so I thought!* She made me mind, respect my elders, go to school, study and do my homework, clean up my room and my bathroom, wash dishes, sweep the floor, vacuum the carpet, dust the furniture, do laundry, rake the leaves and cut the grass. She encouraged me to change my attitude, insisted that I tell the truth regardless of the consequences and insisted that I iron up all of my clothes for the week on the weekend, when I could have been doing something more fun.

She made me keep my promises to others, made me be on time for everything, made me sit quietly at times, and wouldn't let me interrupt her when she was talking, unless it was an emergency. She wouldn't let me hear what she and the other grown ups were talking about, and she wouldn't let me contribute to their conversations, since they weren't talking to me anyway. She felt that information in the hands of a child was dangerous.

She wouldn't let me make C's, D's or F's in school, and insisted that I bring home my books everyday from school. She even bought me a huge book bag to make sure there was plenty of room for all of my books and my homework. I was the only kid in school who took home all of their books everyday! She was so mean she made me sit at the dinner table for hours, doing my homework. I couldn't even watch television until my homework was completed. And when I did loose my mind temporarily, and not study hard enough to make an A or B on a test, she would take away my television and phone privileges! That was torture because then there was nothing to do but read a book.

She wouldn't let me do what I wanted to even when I wasn't in trouble for anything. She wouldn't let me accept money from boys, or have boys over to the house until I was sixteen. She wouldn't let me sit in a boy's car in front of the house, and didn't approve of a boy pulling up outside and blowing his car horn for me to come outside.

She was so mean, she wouldn't let me gossip on the phone with my friends, because she used to say that a dog that will carry a bone, will bring one too. She wouldn't even let me talk back to her when I thought she was wrong, roll my eyes at her when she said something I didn't like, and she had this thing she did with her eyes that got my attention, and let me know she meant business.

You see, my mother was raising me up to be an intelligent, independent young woman, who is a productive member of today's society. Because she was so mean to me, I made good grades in school, got scholarships to colleges and was on the college Deans List, and have written four books, and numerous articles for newspapers and several magazines.

Because she was so mean to me, I know what it is to keep a clean house and groom myself and carry myself as a young woman should. Because she was so mean, I am a dependable, hard working, dedicated and caring young woman who is always on time and knows that there is a time to speak and a time to listen. Because she was so mean, I respect not just my elders: but everyone, because I want them to respect me. Because she was so mean, I never disrespected my parents, who are both gone now, and I demand respect from my children, my granddaughter and the children I am in contact with daily. Because my mother was so mean, I taught my children to be respectful of others, and I require that my children stay in a child's place and not mistake height or size, or a little peach fuzz and bass in their tone for being grown. Because my mother was so mean, I understand now that a "no" didn't mean that I did anything wrong, it just meant that all questions had three answers, yes, no, and we'll see, depending on how she felt that day, and whether the question was in my best interest or a waste of my time. Because my mother was so mean, I used to quiver when young girls called my home late at night for my sixteen-year-old son, and asked me if I knew where he was. It upset me to have to ask those girls if they had been taught phone manners, because when you call someone's home, the correct thing to say to the person on the other end of the phone is, "Hello."

Because my mother was so mean, I don't gossip about others. I try to help others as often as I can, and I have compassion for those who fall on unfortunate times. I try to give people the benefit of the doubt, but use my instincts that God gave me to know when people mean me no good.

I learned a lot from my mother and even though she has passed away, I am reminded of things she taught me daily, especially when it comes to raising my children. Because I am an only child, people thought that I was spoiled. I wasn't spoiled, but I was loved a whole lot. I didn't mind sharing with people, as long as they didn't destroy my things, and I didn't mind listening to my grandparents tell their back-in-the-day stories, because those stories helped me to understand who they were and where my parents came from.

I truly miss my mother, and my father, but the seeds of love and pearls of wisdom that they taught me are carried with me everyday, which allows their spirit to continue to thrive.

I hope that if there are any readers who are on bad terms with their parents, or the people who raised them, that they will take the opportunity to make that relationship right. I tell my children the same thing my grandmother and my mother told me, you only get one mother, the rest are replacements, and no replacement is as good as the real thing.

BUT I STILL DO NOT LIKE TO IRON!!

ONLY YOU CAN MAKE YOU HAPPY

I understand your frustration. You feel as though no one appreciates you or cares about your needs.

Your child keeps getting into trouble, but it's not your fault, because you've given him what he needed to be a productive member of society. You've given him pearls of wisdom and pieces of dreams to help him accomplish obtainable goals. Don't think that he hasn't heard you. No, your words didn't just go in one ear and out the other. They are there, inside his head, on repeat, like a broken record every time he tries to pretend that the wrong choice is easier to live with than the right choice.

Your employer doesn't seem to appreciate your work. He constantly criticizes you and makes you feel worthless. You've contemplated quitting, but can't because the job pays the bills and you've got children to feed, as well. You've wondered what is it that has made this man so impossible to work for. Day in and day out, you've dreaded coming to work. You've taken the long way to work, and sat in your car just a little longer than necessary just getting one last moment of peace, before entering the doors of that dreaded place you call "work".

You've told yourself time and time again that no one should have to work under conditions that cause them stress, accompanied with headaches, body aches and sickness that can only be described as "the feeling you get when you get to work, or think of having to go to work." Just hold on to thoughts of peace. Rest assured, your good work hasn't gone unnoticed, and no one can take away your ability. Not even with words that try to tear down your spirit.

Your spouse doesn't understand you. The communication that was once good is no longer there. You don't talk to each other. You barely look at each other. You sleep on opposite sides of the bed, and don't cross the imaginary line down the middle. You speak only when necessary, and are thankful when time permits you to be away from one another. This didn't happen overnight, but gradually, from little misunderstandings that blossomed into big arguments.

Things can go back to the way they were with a little work. Small conversations can turn into lengthy ones. Words spoken out of need, can be exchanged to words spoken out of love. The key to getting back to the good old days of holding hands and being affectionate is trying.

Your best friend has started treating you differently. She spends less and less time with you, and her conversations with you are merely that. The spirit of sisterly love is no longer felt, and the little things that were once done to show how much the friendship meant, no longer happen. The sad part is, you really don't know what happened. You don't recall saying the wrong thing, or doing the wrong thing. You've always been yourself, the real you that brought the two of you together as friends. You've thought back, to situations and conversations, but can't figure out what it was that ripped up your friendship. Don't continue to worry about it because for every person that exits your life, a new one will enter, and new friendships will emerge.

Remember to value yourself, regardless of what others think or say. In the end, you are your own true best friend. Only you can make yourself truly happy.

BEAUTY IN EVERYONE

A short while ago, I had a conversation with a young woman. She didn't know that she was beautiful, and for a long time she didn't think that her parents liked her. She felt that they loved her out of obligation, but that they really didn't like her because she was different. I explained to this blossoming rose that she was beautiful, not only on the outside, but on the inside as well. I believe that I got through to her, because by the end of our conversation, through a waterfall of tears she thanked me for making her feel special.

It is my belief that parents sometimes get sidetracked with daily activities, and often forget to shower praises on their children. I remember my mom always complimenting me and encouraging me to do great things, and I remember my dad paying me the ultimate compliment when I was about thirteen-years-old. He told me I didn't need to wear make-up because I had natural beauty. That compliment made me feel good, and boosted my self-esteem.

I have children of my own, boys. Although I can not compliment them on less than perfectly cleaned rooms, I try to make up for it by complimenting school work done well, acceptable report cards and positive changes in attitudes and behavior.

Not only is it the responsibility of parents to help boost egos, it is also the responsibility of society to be kind to others. Whether it be a spouse, significant other, a best friend, or a mentor, kind words and deeds help others know that they are appreciated and respected. There is something special and beautiful about each and every person we come in contact with, and it only takes a moment to make a person smile.

Let's explore for a moment the different types of beautiful people.

There's beauty in the person who always has a kind word for others, even when they have the weight of the world on their shoulder.

There's beauty in the person who always has a smile on their face.

There's beauty in the person with the less than perfect shape.

There's beauty in the person who never complains about anything.

There's beauty in the person who is always dependable.

There's beauty in the person who finds joy in helping others.

There's beauty in the minister who leads his congregation.

There's beauty in the person who passes you a peppermint during church on Sunday morning.

There's beauty in the people who volunteer their time to help others, whether at church or in the community.

There's beauty in the person who holds the door open for you at the grocery store so that you can go first.

There's beauty in the person who has faith and determination to complete impossible tasks.

There's beauty in the doctor who prays for his patients.

There's beauty in the cancer patient enduring treatments with grace and poise.

There's beauty in the less than perfect student who tries to get good grades.

There's beauty in the coach who teaches values and morals.

There's beauty in the teacher who teaches because she wants to, not for the money.

There's beauty in the old lady sitting on the park bench with her cats.

There's beauty in the person who wishes you blessings at the end of a phone call.

There's beauty in the single parent who can't find the perfect mate.

There's beauty in the *frog* who doesn't think he'll ever find his princess.

There's beauty in the frustrated father trying to teach his child to ride a bike.

There's beauty in the old man on the corner telling stories of his past.

Awo Osun Kunle said, "You may not know how to raise your self-esteem, but you definitely know how to stop lowering it." For the struggling man or woman who doubts their self-worth, take a look at yourself from the inside out. If you are beautiful on the inside, then there is no doubt that your inner beauty will shine through for others to share on the outside.

SEE MORE BEAUTY

See the beauty in the school crossing guard who demands the safety of pedestrians, in the rain, cold, sleet and sunshine.

See the beauty of the school bus driver who carefully transports students to and fro each day.

See the beauty in the teacher who comes early and stays late to help students get an understanding of schoolwork.

See the beauty in the tutor who calmly repeats directions to the child who doesn't understand his math.

See the beauty in the great-grandmother who transports her great-grandchildren to and from activities daily.

See the beauty in the grandparent helping a toddler to learn.

See the beauty in the parent nervously allowing a teenager to drive for the first time.

See the beauty in the toddler sitting quietly in the church pew mesmerized by the sounds of the musical instruments.

See the beauty in the child who can't hit the ball on the tee. See the beauty in the child who runs the wrong way during the game.

See the beauty in the woman at church who sends out notes of encouragement and love to people when they least expect it.

See the beauty in the person who prays for you.

See the beauty in the mother trying to instill morals and values in her children.

See the beauty in the father who takes the time to play games with his children, and his children's friends.

See the beauty in the person at the grocery store who helps another reach something on a shelf that's too high.

See the beauty in the person in line who allows the person with fewer grocery items to go first.

See the beauty in the elderly couple at the restaurant who stopped at your table as they were leaving to compliment your children for being so well mannered.

See the beauty in the person who flags you down to alert you that your tire is low.

See the beauty in the stranger who smiles at you in passing.

See the beauty in the person who encourages you to do that which you think is impossible.

See the beauty in the person who listens when you need to vent.

See the beauty in the person who throws your newspaper on the sidewalk, rather than in the mud.

See the beauty in the person trying to give directions to someone driving on unfamiliar streets.

See the beauty in the supervisor who has an understanding heart, is lenient when an employee's loved one is sick, and expresses sincere sympathy when a loved one passes away.

James Russell Lowell said, "All the beautiful sentiments in the world weigh less than a single lovely action."

With that thought in mind, see that beauty has nothing to do with outward appearance, but with actions and reactions.

SOLDIERS IN THE LORD'S ARMY

Left. Left. Left. Right. Left.
We are soldiers in the army.
We have to fight, although we have to cry.
We have to hold up the blood stained banner.
We have to hold it up until we…die.

We are soldiers in Army
We do more before 9am, than most people do all day.
We learn respect, honor, pride, commitment, and skill
We learn to walk, fight, survive and improvise
in a different way.

We are soldiers in the Lord's Army
We have to forgive, encourage, intercede,
and watch what we say.
We learn love, charity, peace, faith, hope, understanding
We learn to respect others, appreciate God's blessings and pray, twenty-
four hours a day.

We are soldiers in the Army
We don't always agree with why we are fighting,
Or what we are fighting for.
We take orders and do our best to follow them

Some have lost their lives, for no reason of their own;
It seems to be happening more and more.

We are soldiers in the Lord's Army
We try to follow the commandments God set for us
We strive to reach, teach, and help
Remembering our Christian walk is a must.

We are soldiers in the Army
We wear camouflage to blend in with our surroundings
We wear gear, to protect our head,
And boots to protect our feet.
Our weapons are guns, knives and grenades
In case our enemies we have to defeat.

We are soldiers in the Lord's Army
We wear the truth and the breastplate of righteousness
These are a few pieces of the full armor of God.
Our feet are shod with the gospel of peace;
We wear the shield of faith and the helmet of salvation.
We carry with us the sword of the spirit,
Which is the Word of God.

We are soldiers in the Army
We carry our loved one's close to our hearts
We pray that God returns us safely home
No matter the distance that keeps us apart.

We are soldiers in the Lord's Army
We pray for our enemies, and love others as God loves us.
We show our love for God through our actions and words
No matter what may come, in God we trust.

We are soldiers in the Army
We are soldiers in the Lord's Army
We have to watch, fight and pray…
In order to survive every day.

Left. Left. Left. Right. Left…
Turn the pages of the Bible…
Left. Left. Left. Right. Left.

STAR

Twinkle, little Star!
Shine bright, big Star!
Star that you are-
Wonderful, intelligent, magnificent, Star.
We are friends, we are family
Lovingly, truthfully, differently, respectfully, harmoniously, disagreeably.
Amazing are we!
Not important is the race, color or creed,
Not an issue should our denomination or religion be.
Standing together, with God on our side,
His love for us makes us shine in, and outside.
I'm short. You're tall.
You're big. I'm small.
I'm funny. You're serious.
Sometimes life makes us delirious.
I will love you when times are hard.
I will look past your pain and scars.
I will pray with you when your faith is weak.
I will pray for you when your lips can't speak.
I will embrace our differences.
I won't judge your circumstances.
I will encourage you as you go along life's way.
I will lift you up in prayer each day.
Do you know you are a **STAR**?
Special, **T**errific, **A**mazing, **R**adiant.
Do you know you are a **STAR**?

Saved, **T**riumphant, **A**wesome, **R**emarkable.
Do you know you are a **STAR**?
Sincere, **T**rustworthy, **A**mbitious, **R**egal.
I'm glad you have it all together!
I enjoy our fellowship, through good, and stormy weather.
And even if you didn't let your light glow-
It wouldn't change my feelings,
Because you don't have to be a **STAR** to be in my show.
My show is my world, my life, my heart.
I pray our friendship, our family will never be too far apart.

ABOUT THE AUTHOR

CaSaundra W. Foreman has been writing since she was thirteen years old. Poetry was her first love. Her first article was published in a local newspaper when she was fourteen. She enjoys writing stories and poetry that will encourage and uplift others.

She is the author of *The Determination of I, The Motherless Children* and *When An Angel Takes Flight/The Light.* She has written for *The African Posta, The Waco Tribune Herald, The Brazos News* and the *Anchor News.* Her work has been published in the *Voices of Nature* and *Reflections Magazine* and *Quest Magazine.*

CaSaundra lives in Waco, TX. She is the Youth Director for the Doris Miller Family YMCA. She has two sons, Marquis and LaBraska, and two grandchildren.

Marquis, reading to his daughter, Mya, who is 3 years-old in this picture.

ABOUT THE COVER

The cover was designed by Sherman Howard, III, of Waco, TX. He is the owner of OnTheSpot Grapfx, and has been in business for over fifteen years.

Howard has helped me get the design from inside my head to the covers of three of my books, *The Motherless Children, The Determination of I* and *Read It Again, Please!*

My mother used to read to me, and I read to my sons. Now, we read to Mya, and whenever we finish the story, she always says, *"Read it again, please!"*

The photo on the front was taken when Mya was two years-old, and LaBraska, was sixteen.

That's where the title and cover idea for the book came from.

The Determination

of

by CaSaundra W. Foreman

firmness of purpose; resolve

Haven't picked up your copy of
The Determination of I yet? Here's what people have said about it...

"When I first read *The Determination of I*, I was on my way to Europe and as I started reading, I started to cry. I cried, and would wipe my eyes, then cry some more, then wipe my nose and so on. Remember, all of this is happening on the plane. When I got to the third chapter, I bawled my little eyes out like a baby. I was crying so hard because that story related to me so much! Luckily, the guy next to me is sleeping. The young ladies across the aisle were looking at me, like they were wondering why was I crying. When I noticed what was happening, I had to laugh a little bit as I looked for my tissues. As I read and cried throughout the book, I thought about how much these stories related to me. These stories are occurrences that happen to real people every day. That's why I think other people may relate so well to these stories."-Jasmine S.

"*The Determination of I* is a must read book that is a true illustration of real life conflict. Although not exactly the same problems in every story...I can relate to the pain and the feelings of deception and disrespect that each character in this book is going through. Being a woman of the Lord, I detected that prayer and the Lord are the deciding factor in each story. *The Determination of I* was a real joy to read."-Beverly C.

"*The Determination of I* is a great read. As CaSaundra mentions in her preface, every one has struggles. At times we tend to think that we are alone and are the only ones dealing with the hurdles of life, but this book shows us some of the struggles of others and by seeing that, hopefully we will continue to fight and make it through. I thank God for CaSaundra and for her talent in writing and expression through this compilation of short stories. I would encourage anyone and everyone who is dealing with life's struggles to get a copy of this book, and read it, and share it with others."-Diane L.

"*The Determination of I* has been such an inspirational book for me. Until you are aware of someone else's storm, your storm becomes a beautiful spring day with flowers blooming and birds chirping. Reading this book has given me a brand new insight on my life and how I plan to handle certain situations within my life. I look forward to reading more books written by CaSaundra Foreman."–Tracy S.

"*The Determination of I* is a good read. The book serves up a number of life learning struggles that individuals overcome through a common trait, self determination. The writer's ability to capture the spirit of life lesson statements that are familiar across families is both clever and displays the brilliance of the author's well retained generational wisdom. For anyone that has experienced trials and tribulations, *The Determination of I* is a quaint reminder that we are not alone and we can will ourselves beyond our tests and trials through Christ. This book is a great book club selection, and I am definitely sharing *Sweet Tea* with my daughter! Thank you for *Sweet Tea*!"–Samuel R.

"My wife and I read this book together. We laughed and cried together, and at times, we would look at each other and wonder if the stories were about us, but knew that the author couldn't have known what we had been through. These stories were so believably encouraging. It was refreshing to know that there are other people dealing with issues, and especially behavior problems with their children. We have shared some of the stories with our children, to show them that we aren't the only parent's who demand respect and have rules. *The Determination of I* was definitely uplifting to us. We are encouraging our friends and family to read this book."-Brian & April M.

"I love *The Determination of I*! My favorite story is *They Get on My Nerves*! This book was great!"-India A.

"The book *The Determination of I* made me laugh, cry and think, and then laugh and cry some more. I loved it! I have it on my Kindle, and several of my relatives have it on their Kindles as well. Thank you for making us go through so many different emotions."-Deirdre D.

***

God grant me the **serenity** to accept the things I *cannot* change,
The **courage** to change the things I *can,*
And the **wisdom** to know the difference.
~Serenity Prayer

***

Thank you, Lord, for my many, many blessings!
Amen.
~cwf~